PRAISE FOR *Numamushi*

"This is a work of utter genius. Mesmerizing. Magical. Transportive."

—Eva Wong Nava, author of *The House of Little Sisters*

"*Numamushi* is a hauntingly beautiful tale of friendship, family, healing, and transformation. Mina's lyrical prose and gorgeous storytelling charm the reader in the most delightful way."

— Thersa Matsuura, author of *The Carp-Faced Boy* and creator of the podcast *Uncanny Japan*

NUMAMUSHI

NUMAMUSHI

Mina Ikemoto Ghosh

LANTERNFISH PRESS

PHILADELPHIA

Lanternfish Press
21 S. 11th Street, Office #404
Philadelphia, PA 19107
lanternfishpress.com

Cover Design: Kimberly Glyder
Cover Images: Shutterstock/Dhiraj Gursale, Shutterstock/Graphic
Compressor
Full Page Illustrations: Mina Ikemoto Ghosh
Small Illustratons: Shutterstock/jet

Printed in the United States of America.
27 26 25 24 23   1 2 3 4 5

Library of Congress Control Number: 2023933022
Print ISBN: 978-1-941360-77-4
Digital ISBN: 978-1-941360-78-1

DEDICATION

おばあちゃんへ
長生きしてくれてありがとう

To my parents.
Thank you for your patience.

*U*UMAMUSHI HAD COME to the great white snake from upstream, floating on robes made buoyant with flaming grease. The fire had peeled the baby's skin, burning it red, black, and raw, but when the kind old snake coiled about it, to drown it free of suffering, it put out its tiny tongue and touched it to the snake's cool nose.

The white snake had loved once, long ago and only once. Ever since then, it had lived alone beneath the bridge where the river's scaled waves had carved a hollow. From time to time in the dark of its loneliness, it had reminisced upon the trusting act that was loving, the spring sunlight of it, that could push comfort into the cracks of a long winter's ice.

No one had ever dared ask the great white snake of the river, with his jaws full of venom and his coiling might, for such comfort since. But in that baby's touch, the snake sensed just such a question, and with it the boldest desire to live.

So the snake scrubbed the baby clean of burning jelly and chose to raise it as his own. There was plenty of space in his hollow, and he remembered fondly the comfort of love and the soft joy in tenderly giving it.

"I said to myself, 'This skinless child, this little soft one.'" The white snake told this story the same way each time. "'I will teach him to grow skin anew and to shed it, so that he may never be hurt in this cruel way again. I will call him Numamushi, that he might be at home in the marshes; that thick mud might always hide him when he needs it; that water might always soothe his pains when he asks it; and that the earth hold him close, so the bite of fire will never touch him again.'"

When he was older, Numamushi would ask, "Why don't you have a name, Father?"

"I know what I am, little marshworm, wholly and truly. I do not need a name to remind me or to be called back."

"Then why do I?"

"Humans must have names. They need them to know where, when, and what they are. They get lost easily without them. They are afraid of being lost. Their names are the spells to call them back."

"Am I human?"

"You are, my dear." The white snake fluttered his tongue through Numamushi's hair. "See how you've named me 'Father,' though I do not need it?"

In Father's river, Numamushi grew happy, well-fed, and loved. He learnt how to curl in the cradle of Father's coils, to let winter sink him into sleep, trusting meltwater to coax him awake. He'd shed

2

his skin thirty times by his third summer. By his fourth, he could catch the dark-spotted frogs in the paddies with his own hands. By his fifth, he hunted between and beneath the human houses, slipping unseen along the irrigation ditches, and could loosen his jaw to swallow rats whole, just as Father taught him.

Father listened to the tales of his adventures with a proud gleam in his mirror eyes.

There was only one place in Father's land that Numamushi didn't go. That was the house closest to Father's bridge. It was separated from the river by a paddy and wild patch of grass. Its walls were sun-blackened, its tiles cracked. Old long-legged wasps' nests hung in grey blisters under its eaves and glossy ivy covered its sides. In the autumns, golden orb-weaver spiders draped webs in sheets between the buildings, and in the summers, the wild grass lit up with flowers in orange and pink.

In his fourth summer, Numamushi had picked a handful and taken them to Father to know their name.

"Those are zinnias, my dear." Suddenly, Father recoiled. "Little marshworm, where did you find these?"

"In the grass by the dark house."

"The dark house!"

"Why, Father? Is the land there bad?"

Father shuddered. "It is poison to me."

"But you're the white snake of the river. Haven't you the most powerful poison in this land?"

"True, my little one, the deadliest. But all my venom would not protect me from the poison of the dark house."

Fearful of the fear he saw in Father's mirror-bright eyes, Numamushi let the current pull the zinnias out of his hands, up and away to the river surface above their heads. "Should I not go there anymore?"

"You can go wherever you wish, but bring me nothing from the dark house. Tell me, did you see anyone there?"

Numamushi had not. The dark house had been empty as long as he'd known it. "Should I watch it in case someone does come to it?"

Silence sat as a water snail in Numamushi's ear. Father nodded. "That would please your father very much."

From then on, Numamushi watched the dark house from a distance.

I N NUMAMUSHI'S SIXTH SUMMER, a light appeared in the dark house, small and zinnia-orange, unfurling after sunset.

The following dawn, there were humans. They plucked at the tiles and peeled off the ivy like last season's skin. The wasps' nests came down. Gleaming sickles cut the wild grass down into ankle-deep scrub.

Numamushi watched from the riverbank, enthralled by the noise and gleefully catching the mice fleeing from the building. The days passed. The drained paddy was refilled. The humans vanished.

Except for one.

For the first few days, they were a tall silhouette in the distance, sweeping their courtyard and hanging out clothes to dry. They dressed every day in brown hitoes and grey hakamas that made Numamushi think of wet earth and rainfall. They were quiet. Unlike the ivy-skinners and tile-pluckers, they didn't climb about the house or make it clatter.

After five days of watching, Numamushi swam into the paddy. He meant to hide amidst the rice and get a closer look at the new neighbor, but when he lifted his head out of the water, he immediately ducked below again, for there were bare feet at the paddy's edge.

The dark house's human gazed out over the paddy. Their eyes skated over the mountain, alighted on the river, paused on the bridge, then settled on the paddy itself.

Those eyes met Numamushi's.

Numamushi flinched, and fled.

He'd been seen!

No human had ever looked at Numamushi like that. Father's power and his own skill meant that any human who saw him dismissed Numamushi as a shadow, the wind on the water at most.

But this human had truly seen him.

Stranger still, behind their thin-framed glasses...

...there had been a snake's mirror gleam in their sharp human eyes.

*M*AYBE NUMAMUSHI should have been wary of the new neighbor. Maybe those eyes should've been his clue to leave them well alone. Instead, he returned to the paddy, day after day, drawn irresistibly by this new thrilling game of, maybe, being seen.

This human found him every time. They would raise their head and look Numamushi's way, spotting him whether he was in the paddy or the trees or amongst the earth turned up for the new allotment, however still he made himself.

After days of scurrying back to the bridge, the thrill of the game soured to shame. Numamushi was Father's son in Father's land. He shouldn't be so easily found. The tenth time he was spotted, he kicked mud out of the paddy as he fled, throwing it into the human's face.

The next day, Numamushi ventured out of the paddy, up the flight of steps, and dared to enter the dark house's yard. This time, he would not leave. The dark-house human would leave first.

He hid behind a persimmon tree. The human sat on the veranda, fanning smoke over a small grill where two fishes were popping with fat.

After a while, they looked towards the persimmon tree.

"I've always been good at spotting little animals," they said, pushing their glasses up their nose. "It's the heartbeat that gives you away. If you're wondering."

Their voice was deep with a lyrical, meandering flow from one word to the next, as if they—he—spoke with river water.

He held out a hand. "Come out, my rude little mud-kicking neighbor. Come out, come out."

He made a clicking noise with his tongue. Numamushi turned up his nose. He would not be coaxed out like the neighborhood tomcat. To make his point, he left the tree with a loud fart and snapped a few of its branches as he went.

The man laughed. It was only when Numamushi was back

at the bridge that he realized he'd lost his own game and left before the dark-house human after all.

"Did the man at the dark house do something today?" Father asked when Numamushi ripped apart a diving beetle more savagely than necessary. "Did he hurt you?"

"No, Father." But Numamushi hadn't told Father about the dark house's new occupant yet. "Father, how did you know that it's a man there?"

"Your father knows things."

Numamushi frowned.

Father nosed the wrinkle between Numamushi's eyebrows smooth. "Be careful how you play with him, my dear."

"Why?"

"Your father knows things."

Sometimes Father would say the words *your father* with great care, as though they were sharper than his fangs and could cut the inside of his mouth.

He didn't tell Numamushi to keep away from the man.

THERE WERE VOICES at the dark house. The door of the room overlooking the yard was open. The man's watery voice rose clear and curling.

Numamushi crept from the persimmon's shadow to peer over the veranda's edge.

The man was not alone. Four women, whom Numamushi recognized from the nearby houses, knelt at a row of low tables. At the man's words, they nodded and traced sticks over thin leaves of paper, smearing them with clinging black fluids that dried like blood.

The lines laid down on the paper glistened. Danced. Numamushi thought of the "writing" that Father had first shown him on the side of a discarded candy tin.

The man noticed Numamushi, of course. Or heard his heartbeats, if he was to be believed. He looked up and Numamushi glowered back, willing his gaze to convey that this sharp-eared man shouldn't get so cocky.

The corners of the man's mouth turned up. He looked away to continue attending to the women and cooled himself with a paper fan.

That was all the acknowledgment Numamushi received until the women left, gifting the man with sweet potatoes, daikon, and onions as they went. Sunset had painted the mountain red, and the crickets were shrilling in the allotment's boundary brush.

The man rose from his desk. Numamushi retreated swiftly to the persimmon tree.

"Still playing our game?" The man stopped on the veranda and looked out from the house's shadow. "You know that sore losers only hurt themselves, hm?"

Numamushi bit his tongue. If he spoke, he would lose this game for good.

"You're careful with your words." The man smiled. "That's good. Words are water, after all, and water is precious. Easily wasted. I've something for you." He took something out of his sleeve. "Better than a fish, isn't it?"

A tree frog sat squarely on the man's palm. Plump, brilliant green, it blinked in the evening sunlight. The man held the frog out towards the persimmon tree. "You must be hungry if you've been sitting there watching me all day."

Numamushi's stomach rumbled. He killed his breath and stayed so still that a red dragonfly landed on his shoulder.

After a while, the man shrugged. "Well, if you don't want it, I'm not going to waste it."

He lifted the frog to his mouth and swallowed the surprised creature whole.

The man's throat bulged. Skin and ridges of cartilage stretched about the frog's kicking legs and then contracted, pushing the lump below his robe collar, out of sight.

Numamushi scowled. How cruel. How mean. Now all he could think about was how soft tree frogs were and of the meatiness of their legs. He gnawed his tongue. He would not give in.

"Fine, fine. You're a stubborn one." The man took another frog from his sleeve, as slow-blinking and stunned as the last. He placed it on the veranda. "If you come back tomorrow, this neighborly *oniisan* will have frogs for you again."

The man turned away.

He was leaving first! Numamushi had outlasted him! The game was his!

With a hoot of triumph, Numamushi darted from his hiding place and stuffed the frog into his cheek.

The frog barely gave a kick. It had been charmed, which annoyed Numamushi deeply. Father hadn't charmed prey into calmness since Numamushi was two, when his little snatching hands had been slower than his food. However,

Numamushi was hungry, and as the winner of the day's game, it was only natural that he deserved a sweet prize.

He'd take this sleepy, charmed frog.

*B*UT IT WASN'T FROGS or victory that disturbed Numamushi's sleep that night; it was the trailing black lines those women had been scraping on their leaves.

They wriggled behind his eyes, fresh and glistening, like tadpoles, slugs, and eels. They followed him into the morning with a feeling like he had spotted a new frog in the paddy and didn't know its name.

He wanted to know its name.

Father said that the man's sessions were called "classes." The next time the man had a class, Numamushi didn't watch him but watched the women in their faded *monpe*, tracing that wriggling writing with their tufted sticks onto paper leaves.

He listened to the scraping licks of their strokes, thought of the river touching its banks, and didn't realize the day had passed until the women left and the man stood from his table.

Numamushi ducked under the veranda.

The planks creaked above him. "Are you interested more in my classes now than me?"

Numamushi didn't know how to answer that.

Hands appeared in the gap between the veranda and the ground. In the left was a dark-spotted frog, in the right a wrinkled one. Charmed to calmness, they huddled sleepily in the man's palms. "I did promise. Go on."

The left hand dropped the dark-spotted frog.

Numamushi's hand snapped out, catching and shoveling the frog into his mouth before it could hit the ground and get away.

The man laughed.

"My name is Mizukiyo." He opened and closed the fingers of his right hand, winking the wrinkled frog. "Come out from under there. Ah!" He pulled the frog back from Numamushi's instinctive grab. "You can have it after introductions. What's your name?"

The land and its creatures all knew *what* they were and didn't care so much for *who*. It was only humans who asked for names and gave them to everything they feared to lose.

Nobody had asked Numamushi's name before. Buoyed on the thrill of novelty, he answered: "Numamushi."

"Come out from there, Numamushi."

How strange to have this name said aloud in a stranger's voice, and a voice that didn't seem so strange at all. The river of it had the same shadows and twists as Father's.

Numamushi crawled out. The man, Mizukiyo, knelt on the veranda, patting the wrinkled frog. Numamushi hadn't been mistaken. There was a film of mirror in his eyes, just like in Father's, a shifting silver sheen like moonlight on water.

In Father's eyes the mirror gleam was gentle. In Mizukiyo's eyes it was tired. He'd looked as if he'd played too many games, even after giving up on winning them.

"Numamushi," said Mizukiyo. "A muddy name for a muddy boy. Here." When Numamushi hung back from taking the frog, Mizukiyo raised his eyebrows. "We're only five years out of a war, little one. There isn't food to waste. Very well. This *oniisan's* got to think for his own stomach."

He lifted the frog to his own mouth. Numamushi lunged for Mizukiyo's hand, and whilst he got the frog, Mizukiyo got Numamushi. He caught him by the collar and reeled him onto the veranda. Mouth full of kicking frog, Numamushi couldn't even shout as Mizukiyo dragged him up.

"What are your clothes made of?" Mizukiyo examined the folds of Numamushi's clothes with fascination. "They look like snakeskin."

Numamushi swallowed the frog. "Father's skin sheddings."

"Your father?"

He nodded with pride and pointed past the persimmon tree, over the allotment and paddy to the river. Unlike Numamushi's sheddings, Father's retained the smooth suppleness of living skin, its moon-white coloring, and traces of his power. Father had made many robes for Numamushi over the years. They clung tight when he needed to fit down pipes and never caught or tore. "My father knows things."

"Your father..." Mizukiyo's eyes narrowed. "I don't doubt it."

"What about your clothes? Did your father shed them?"

"No, they're cotton. From a plant that grows rabbit-tails. Have you ever eaten a rabbit?" Numamushi hadn't and felt young and small to admit it, especially when he could still taste that charmed frog. "I suppose you don't find them often about the paddies. No matter. Their tails stick in your throat. How long have you lived with your father?"

"Six summers."

"Ah, so you can count."

"Father taught me numbers."

"What a dedicated father, making clothes and teaching numbers," said Mizukiyo in a strange tone. "What of letters? I can hear that 'Father' has taught you words."

"No letters, but Father has taught me lots!" Numamushi wouldn't have this man think Father was anything but the best of teachers. "He tells me the names of things. He taught me how to catch my food, and how to hide, and how to sleep through the winter, and shed my skin."

"You can shed your skin?"

"It's easy. Can't you?"

"Not as easily as some. He must be very loving, to teach you everything you ask of him."

Numamushi grimaced. "Not everything."

"Oh?"

"He won't teach me how to make venom." If only Numamushi had poison like Father's, maybe he wouldn't feel so scared about the bigger humans when they stepped too close to his hiding places. "Father says it isn't right for me. He says humans don't make poison in their mouths."

"Ha!" Mizukiyo let out a sharp bark of laughter that made Numamushi jump and startled the sparrows into flight. "Your father's quite right!"

Numamushi frowned, looking at Mizukiyo closely. "But you have poison, don't you?"

"What makes you say that?"

"You look like you do."

Mizukiyo had a triangular face with a pointed chin and a short, blunt nose. There was a hard fullness to his cheeks, a roundedness like a mamushi's, that Father had warned Numamushi came from venom pockets.

Numamushi had regarded such rounded cheeks with envy when he was little. "So, do you have poison? Can you teach me?"

"Your father said it himself. It's not human to have poison," Mizukiyo replied. Numamushi grumbled, folding his arms across his chest. It wasn't fair. Did they all want him to be small and scared forever? Then, softer, Mizukiyo went on, "He was correct in his decision. A venomous human would be a cursed thing from the moment he first opened his mouth."

"Cursed?" Numamushi did not know this word.

"But I can teach you letters, or at least symbols." The mirror gleam in Mizukiyo's eyes seemed gentler. "How would you like that, Numamushi? Would you like to know some letters?"

"Is that what you were teaching them?" Numamushi pointed at the low desks, where drying black fluid oozed a lightning-struck cedar smell.

"That's right. Calligraphy. I was teaching them to draw words...oh, you don't understand drawing, do you? Then imagine that your voice, the sound of your thoughts, in your mind, could be made to leave tracks on snow. For others to follow."

"Why would you want others to follow? They'd steal your food."

"It's not stealing if the tracks were left for them on purpose.

It's sharing." Mizukiyo ruffled Numamushi's hair, flicking it out of his eyes like Father did with his tongue. "You're an odd boy. Come back tomorrow. I'll have another frog for you."

Numamushi whooped, then remembered himself. "Don't charm it this time!"

"Don't charm—?"

"I'm not a baby. I don't need my frogs sleepy to eat them. I bet I could catch a frog faster than you could in the water!"

"I'm sure you could." Mizukiyo's gaze went to the river. "All right. No more sleepy frogs. They'll be scared pissless in my sleeves before I give them to you."

"Promise?"

"I promise. Go on, Numamushi. Go home to your father."

FATHER WAS WAITING FOR HIM, the wedge of his head anxiously skimming just below the water's surface. Once Numamushi had followed him down to their hollow, Father's tongue flicked over Numamushi's clothes where Mizukiyo had grabbed him.

"Did he give you a name?"

"Do I get a new name from every human I meet?"

"No, no, I meant his name. What was his name, little one? Of the boy come to live in the dark house?"

It felt strange for Numamushi to think of Mizukiyo as a boy, but he supposed that Father was as old as the river, and everything in his land was young to him. He told Father everything that had passed between him and Mizukiyo.

"A cursed thing? Is that what he said? Precisely his words?"

"Yes, Father. What did Mizukiyo mean? What is *cursed*?"

The water stirred around the tip of Father's tail. "It's the anger of something forgotten."

"Like a ghost?"

"Almost, little marshworm. If a ghost is a nameless memory of a person, named through remembrance, a curse is a nameless pain of a deed, named through being known. For pain to be known, it must be felt." Father looked up at the river, rushing overhead. "Snakes do not curse each other. Naming things means little to us. But humans may curse us, just as they can name us, like you named me. My dear, what's wrong?"

Numamushi had thrown his arms around Father's neck. "I'll never curse you."

"Little marshworm." Father's water voice softly filled the dark. "If I'd caused you pain and forgotten it, then I would readily accept any curse of yours. I'd justly deserve to suffer it."

*S*UMMER GREW WITH THE RICE. Its light settled in the fresh green of new stems. Its heat gathered in the humid air and pooled on the paddy surfaces.

Numamushi visited Mizukiyo every day. Mizukiyo never gave him a charmed frog again, instead letting them hop about the yard for Numamushi to catch. His own, Mizukiyo kept half-asleep until he tossed them down his throat.

They played games. Mizukiyo would catch a mouse, mark its back with ink, then re-release it into the allotment. The one who caught the mouse again before sunset won it as their prize. Numamushi almost always won these games, and when he didn't, Mizukiyo gave the mouse to Numamushi anyway. They played hide and seek once, then never again. Mizukiyo couldn't even pretend that looking for Numamushi was difficult.

Some days Mizukiyo taught calligraphy in a "primary school" and was away from the house. School, so Mizukiyo told Numamushi, was a place where human children could be put together and watched like frogs in a pot, whilst their parents were busy.

The thought of frogs in a pot gave Numamushi the idea of collecting and storing frogs for their games, which he did—in a hole, dug at the foot of the persimmon tree. That way, when Mizukiyo didn't have time to hunt for himself, they could play as soon as he returned. Numamushi would snack during the school days in a storehouse four paddies downriver, where the humans had laid down sticky strips of tape on the floor and caught mice that made for a quick, easy meal.

On other days, when Mizukiyo held classes in the house, Numamushi would watch and wait patiently for him to finish.

He had learnt to be patient the hard way. Once, fed up with peering over the veranda and itching as the symbols called slugs and eels to mind, Numamushi had found a small nest of long-legged wasps, charmed the wasps quiet, and rolled it into the classroom.

The class had upended into a chaos of flying stone trays, splatters of writing blood, and shrieking locals, before Mizukiyo had re-charmed the wasps and carried the nest out into the paddy.

The look Mizukiyo shot at Numamushi's hiding place that day had sent him fleeing back to the bridge, tears pricking his eyes, but that hadn't been the worst of it. When he'd slunk wretchedly back on Father's insistence that he apologize and take whatever Mizukiyo dealt him, Mizukiyo had had his punishment ready.

"A curse?"

Mizukiyo had given him an odd look before thrusting a wet rag at him. "No. An education."

In cleaning a human house.

After an afternoon of coaxing ink from tatami and polished wood, Numamushi made a solemn oath never to disturb a calligraphy class again. He said nothing of this oath to Mizukiyo, but maybe something of his sentiment got through. At the end of it, Mizukiyo's gaze was less venomous, and he rewarded Numamushi with a plump mouse and fistful of crickets. How lucky Numamushi was that he lived in the river and never needed to clean anything but himself!

He learned that Mizukiyo liked to eat frogs and lizards but not mice, because their fur scratched in his throat. Mizukiyo's ears were sharp, enough that he could track down a wrinkled frog burrowed three feet into the allotment earth. He couldn't hide in mud and water like Numamushi, but he didn't wish to, because he liked to keep his *hitoe* and hair pristine and clean. He moved like a human, but when he sat on the veranda or at the front of his class, he had Father's perfect, coiled, watchful stillness.

Sometimes Mizukiyo showed Numamushi his students' symbols and Numamushi looked and listened with the feeling of being dangled a fat frog he didn't know the name of. The thought of being able to write, to tell somebody where the food was, that they were important enough he'd want them to know so that they stayed alive too, was new to him. It made him nervous, so he kept his curiosity behind his teeth and watched Mizukiyo's students come and go.

The students dwindled with the weeks. Perhaps, like Numamushi, they'd only approached Mizukiyo out of curiosity about their new neighbor. If that was so, he wondered why Mizukiyo didn't simply coax them with frogs to stay, talk, and play games like he did with Numamushi.

"And waste good frogs on them?" Mizukiyo had scoffed— but only after a hesitation, and it occurred to Numamushi that he hesitated often when it came to talking about other humans. "We're five years out of a war, Numamushi."

"I don't know what that means."

"It means that it would hurt both me and you to waste frogs on people who won't appreciate them."

Numamushi couldn't disagree with that, so he asked no more, though Father told him that shrinking classes for a human teacher were not a good thing. In the days that followed, he clean forgot about Mizukiyo's classes, because it was at last time for his summer shedding.

Numamushi was becoming bigger and less a child. In his excitement to show this off, Numamushi left the river and went running to the dark house with his old skin still hanging in ribbons off his limbs.

He heard a new voice, one that belonged to neither

Mizukiyo nor a student, and quickly hid behind the persimmon.

"...I can't believe you really did it. You really went and tracked down your family house! A grand old thing too!"

"You didn't see the termite extermination bill."

"And I never want to. Numbers still give me nightmares."

The man with Mizukiyo wore a sandy coat, a white shirt, and dark trousers held up by straps. Where Mizukiyo was narrow and angular, this man was wide and square. His forehead wide, his shoulders square. His smile wide, the firm planting of his feet on the ground square. Beside Mizukiyo's long dark thatch, even the cut of his hair looked square.

The two men sat together on the veranda. The stranger held a cup and looked about the yard. He didn't see Numamushi. "This suits you better than priesting."

"You think so?"

"Kiyo, you never liked people very much. As a gentleman of leisure, now you get to be reclusive and irresponsible, and because you're rich, people will call that eccentric and let you be, and you'll still be on their list of eligible neighborhood bachelors, even when you're a bona fide calligraphy obsessive. Oi!" The man nudged Mizukiyo with his elbow when Mizukiyo laughed. "I'm being serious. Temple orphan to hot retired priest is an achievement. What's so funny?"

"There are rumors about me already, Tora."

"Well, you can't drift into a small town out of nowhere without them."

"They're saying I'm cursed."

Numamushi pricked up his ears.

Tora reached over and smacked Mizukiyo on the knee. "If you are, then so am I. And every one of us who set foot out of this country. We'd all deserve it too, a good old curse!"

"I don't mean the war. This house stood empty for twenty-five years. A large property like this, with space that could have been put to use for growing and storing rice and grain, and they decided to just leave it to rot. What do you think, Tora? What do you think happened here that no one would dare touch it?"

Tora's smile shrank. "I like thinking about that as much as I like our Meriken fish-shit top brass."

"Yet you beat Arida in thirteen moves at Go."

"That's different."

"Of course it is." Mizukiyo looked out from the veranda, past the paddy to the river. "Twenty-five years ago, my grandparents were murdered. In this very room behind us."

Tora lowered his cup. "Where you're teaching?!"

"Why not?"

Tora let out a low, jittery laugh, like the skittering of a startled beetle, but Mizukiyo continued to stare over the land to the bridge and the river.

Tora wiped his forehead with his sleeve. "Do you...know who did it?"

"Yes."

"They...in prison?"

"They're dead."

"They...died in prison?"

"Does that matter?"

"Kiyo, I'm trying to work out how haunted and cursed this house, and possibly you, might be."

"She died in childbirth."

Tora looked over his shoulder into the house's shadows, the dark of it, then took a deep breath. "Do you remember what we promised back in Burma?"

Mizukiyo stiffened. "To watch that we both stayed human."

"And that if there was a curse to be had, we'd share it." Tora lowered his voice. "We'd live the curse together."

A large fly buzzed against Numamushi's ear, wings humming low and flat.

"I told you I was born and raised at the temple."

"You did."

"Mizobata, the priest there, was a friend of my mother's from childhood. The night I was born, he came to this house. He knew my mother was due to give birth to a child of unknown parentage, and she'd written to him for solace. Her letters suddenly stopped, so he came to visit her." Mizukiyo gripped his cup. "He found her breaking her jaw open, trying to swallow her parents' remains whole."

"Kiyo..."

"Not even trying to cut them up into bite-sized pieces, but swallowing them from the feet. Like a snake. Until she got impatient and started ripping. She'd killed them. Out of hunger. She told him so. She was desperately hungry and they were there. Easy, slow, accessible prey."

"Was Mizobata on the Philopon at all?"

"Mizobata told the police he'd found my grandparents

being mauled by stray dogs. They never questioned it. He took my mother back to the temple. Somehow, he persuaded her to go with him, and that was where she died." Mizukiyo ignored Tora, staring fixedly at the river. "And there was me."

"And you believe Mizobata's story?"

Mizukiyo gripped his cup tightly, his fingers like biting fangs.

Tora frowned. "Kiyo, why did you buy this place? Why would you choose to live here, believing all that?"

"Because maybe, Tora, it's like you said."

"What did I say?"

"Maybe it suits me more than being a prison chaplain. I feel at home here. You can see that, can't you?"

"Listen, Kiyo." Tora covered his cup, stopping Mizukiyo from refilling it. "You know the saying: Don't touch the gods, and the gods won't touch you."

"If I'm cursed, it's an inheritance I deserve." Tora opened his mouth, but Mizukiyo laughed, cutting across him. "I don't understand why you pretend to be stupid."

Tora smiled slightly. "Easy. Stupid survives."

"But why pretend to be something you're not?"

"Nobody cares about what you think if they think you don't think. You heard the news, didn't you? The Eels Declaration? They've gone for the comrades in the universities. Businesses and communications will follow, fish-shit as they all are."

"Will you be—?"

"I've sold sticky tape door-to-door with my mouth taped shut. I'm dumb. Head empty. I'll be fine."

"Really?"

"All right, amendment: fine, on a condition." Tora dropped his hand to Mizukiyo's shoulder, gripped it. "Don't leave me here, Kiyo, you got me? Don't disappear from my world. Satou and Kuwabara? Gone. Handa and Yamamoto? Up to their eyeballs in Philopon. The way their minds have checked out, their bodies will be following soon. You're the only one left for me. The only one. Tell me that I can count on you sticking around."

"At this house?"

"If it has to be." Tora looked at the house like he could smell the poison in it. "If this is what's keeping you going, I won't judge you for what happened here or what you think your ma did. There's a little bit of that in everyone, from what I've seen. Didn't the war show us that enough? We'll be at it again soon, I bet." When Mizukiyo said nothing, Tora bowed his head. "Please, Kiyo. I spent this much on train tickets from Osaka to find you out here. Borrowed half from the landlady too. Just. Give me this, so that I can go home with other people's money well spent. Tell me you won't leave."

The water of Mizukiyo's voice was gentle. "I'll be here."

"For how long?"

"As long as this skin lasts."

"What does that mean?"

"Don't worry." Mizukiyo put his own hand over Tora's. His eyes were dark, the mirror gleam hidden. "I'm at this house to be haunted and cursed. Dead men can't be either."

"WHO WAS HE?" Numamushi asked when Tora was gone.

Mizukiyo paused in the shadow of the house. "Morifuchi Torajiro. An old friend. Family, of a kind."

"A friend?"

"Someone who makes you feel real and not a ghost."

"I know what friends are." Numamushi pursed his lips, suddenly sheepish. "What's family?"

"As you and your father."

"He's your—?"

"No! Good grief, no!" Mizukiyo cleared his throat and resettled his glasses. "All right. Tora's someone in whose company I feel it doesn't matter if I'm real or a ghost. He's someone to share sad things with."

"Like curses?"

Mizukiyo didn't respond. He settled into a sunlit patch on the veranda and tucked his hands into his sleeves. Numamushi waited for a frog. Instead, Mizukiyo simply shook, like a stiff winter stem rattled by a sudden wind.

Numamushi crawled closer. "Are you cold?"

A shining line ran down the side of Mizukiyo's face.

Father had always encouraged Numamushi to cry freely. If snakes had venom to fill and protect the stomachs that made them snakes, then humans had tears to protect and clean the hearts that made them humans. Both were gifts from the earth and heavens.

"Did he steal your frogs? Shall I go and bite his ankles?"

That drew a laugh from Mizukiyo. "No, Numamushi. No frogs. No ankles. I just wasn't prepared to see him today.

That's all. And I don't do well with ambushes. You can remember that for the next game we play."

Tears flowed down his cheeks and between his words.

"I don't think family is very good for you if it makes you sad," Numamushi said, resolving to bite Tora somewhere that wasn't an ankle the next time he came.

"Ah, no, you're quite right. Family shouldn't make you sad. They'd quite forfeit the designation if that was the case. But they share, Numamushi. They share everything, especially the sad things." Bone creaked as Mizukiyo twisted his fingers together. "If Tora wished to share a curse, I wouldn't be able to stop him—and I'm not good enough of a man to perhaps even wish to."

"What about frogs?"

"What about them?"

"We share frogs. And we share words when we talk." Numamushi climbed onto the veranda where Tora had sat moments earlier. "You could teach me letters, so I'll know how to leave a track for you to find frogs, and I could teach you how to swallow mice, so that the hairs don't tickle. There. We share lots. Can we be family?"

Cicadas mewed in the trees. Mizukiyo hung his head. He twisted his hands like he wanted to coil up under a stone but couldn't make himself small enough.

"It's a strange thing," he said. "If I'd met you even a year ago, I'd have shuddered at the thought of someone like you existing. Yet now, now that I've decided that none of it matters, that their world is one I mustn't be a part of, and that I just want one last summer where I can be everything I've always been told I mustn't be, here I am, eating frogs, catching mice, talking about shedding skin, with you, as if these are all perfectly normal things for a pair of humans to do."

"But it is," Numamushi corrected, because they both could weep and both were human, so all that they did was human too. Father said so. "Isn't it?"

The wind shifted, bending the rice in soft waves towards the river.

Mizukiyo smiled. Numamushi was pleased to see the gentle mirror gleam return to his eyes. Then those eyes stretched wide. "What's wrong with your arms?"

"My arms? Oh!" Numamushi held them up them happily. "Look, Mizukiyo, I'm shedding my skin today!"

"You were out under the sun whilst your arms were still shedding and your new skin was still soft. You're redder than a boiled octopus!" Mizukiyo wiped his eyes with his hands and straightened. "Into the house at once. Let's put some cold cloths on you."

After Numamushi had grudgingly accepted the towels soaked in cold water and the notion that, perhaps, it wasn't all bad to have help peeling the fiddliest pieces of skin away, Mizukiyo opened a tin of white peaches. Dividing it up into two glass bowls, he instructed Numamushi to let the peaches sit on his tongue to taste them, rather than swallowing them down.

The tinned peaches came in "syrup," which was a honey as clear as fresh rain. They had the slipperiness of wet newts and were almost as tasty as freshly frightened tree frogs.

FATHER KEPT NUMAMUSHI in the bridge's shadow for two days. He said it was punishment for imposing on Mizukiyo's kindness when he should've stayed hidden for his shedding.

"So his mother was taken to a temple," Father said, "and died there in childbirth. Ah, no wonder. No wonder!"

"No wonder what?"

Father pressed his nose into Numamushi's hair. "Let's sit in the shallows tonight."

As the white snake pulled him close, Numamushi thought that Father and Mizukiyo might get along. If their sadnesses were scraped across paper, they would leave the same black tracks in the writing blood.

From the shallows they could see the summer stars. The speckled gleam in Father's mirror eyes looked much like tears, if only snakes could cry.

"I'VE BEEN PUTTING THIS OFF, haven't I?" Mizukiyo said, beckoning Numamushi into the house. "It's time I shared some symbols with you. I know a few you might like. Come in and sit down."

Mizukiyo had prepared one of the low writing desks in his classroom.

He showed Numamushi how to grind a dark stick of writing blood into its tray. It made a soothing, circular sound, like the rush of the river over the riverbed, and Numamushi liked it very much. The brush, which Mizukiyo instructed him how to hold and dip, smelled of weasel, which Numamushi liked

less, but when he set the ink to the paper and daubed his first line, blotchy and wriggling, a warm elation blossomed in his chest.

"An eel!"

"Then this is what your name looks like." Mizukiyo smiled too as he took up his own brush. "In slugs and eels."

Mizukiyo showed Numamushi his name in symbols (沼虫), and taught him how to draw it. Then he drew his own name (水清) and let Numamushi compare the two.

"In our land's language, your name's second symbol has come to mean insects. There are theories, however, that once, in the land where this symbol came from, it meant a wholly different thing." Mizukiyo drew something shaped more like a tadpole, with a large head and a long crooked tail. "What do you think, Numamushi? Does this look like a snake?"

Numamushi looked at the picture this way and that. He shook his head.

"Well, one theory is that this symbol represents a snake, and so the second symbol of your own name, Numamushi, which comes from this picture, was in fact once a snake."

"Like Father?" Numamushi looked at his name with new delight.

"Yes, like Father," Mizukiyo replied after a pause. "In China—the land where these symbols came from—this symbol," he pointed at the tadpole, "was found carved into tortoiseshell and deer bone, on tools people think were used for divination."

"What's that?"

"It's how people used to tell if a man was cursed."

Numamushi's skin prickled. He pushed another sheet of paper under Mizukiyo's brush. "Show me the drawing for 'Father'!"

With the symbol freshly drawn on a clean page, Numamushi returned to the river, eager to share his knowledge with the white snake.

His clothes kept the sheet dry until he unfolded it in the hollow, whereupon the paper crumbled in the water and the current swept it away.

"That's all right, little one." Father laughed upon seeing Numamushi's disappointment. "I know what it looks like."

"No, you don't." Numamushi folded his arms. "You don't know what it looks like when I draw it. And everyone's tracks are different. You taught me that about the frogs and the mice. Mizukiyo says it's the same with letters." Numamushi looked up at Father's silvery chin. "You and Mizukiyo say a lot of the same things."

"Do we?"

"Sometimes he sounds like you, too, like the river, and sometimes, the way he looks..." *To the bridge and the river,* Numamushi didn't say, the words sticking as Father's gaze bored into him. *He looks towards the bridge like you look towards the house. With the same eyes.* "He's got mirror eyes, Father! Just like yours."

"Oh, does he?"

"Yes! And I think you'd like him! He'd definitely like you. Father!" An idea struck him. "I want him to be family. If you were his father too, then I'd share you with him. Wouldn't that make us family? Couldn't you—"

"Do you think he's happy, Numamushi?"

Numamushi closed his mouth. He thought about it, hard. He didn't think anyone who lived in that dark house could be "happy," exactly.

"He has food. I get food for him when he doesn't." Numamushi immediately felt that wasn't what Father had wanted to hear. "Father, is Mizukiyo cursed?"

"Why do you ask this?"

"Has it got something to do with the poison in the dark house's land?"

Father hissed, bristling so that his coils crowded the hollow and the bridge's shadow. "Please do not speak of that, my dear."

"Then—"

"Mizukiyo is not cursed." Relief burst bright as a zinnia in Numamushi's heart, but it was short-lived, as Father went on, "But there is a curse. In his skin. Not a curse upon him but a curse to be delivered by him."

"To who?"

"To me."

Numamushi stared into the mirror eye that was only a little smaller than his own face. "Why?"

"Because Mizukiyo's mother suffered greatly, and not only did I not know of it, I never thought to find out. I didn't know she was with child. One night she promised to share this hollow of mine in the river, but she never returned to the bankside. The window she'd always left open for me was boarded and locked, and it stayed that way every night after. I thought she didn't want to know me anymore, that she'd

chosen the human husband her parents had found her, so I
let her be. I left her at the mercy of her parents, it seems." The
river of Father's words flowed dark and curdled with sadness.
"She must have believed I'd forgotten her, but I never did, I
never could. That's how I recognized the taste of her poison in
the land and in the skin of our son. Both carry the fragrance
of her heart, all that fear, pain, and loneliness that she wishes
me to know the name of. It's her curse, meant for me." Father
rocked Numamushi gently. "The moment I set foot on the
land of that house and look upon that boy's face, I will die."

"No!" Numamushi wrapped his arms around Father's head.
He pressed his face against the white cheek with its pouch of
venom. "I don't want you to die. You can't die."

"Don't tell Mizukiyo what I just told you."

"I won't," Numamushi said, even as a diving beetle of a
thought rose at the back of his mind: Family shares everything.

Something told Numamushi that Mizukiyo already knew.
That was why he always stayed on the veranda, gazing out
at the river, instead of walking out along the little dirt track
to the bridge. He knew he carried something in his skin and
didn't want to decide what to do with it. Yet.

"I think he *wants* to meet you," Numamushi said.

Father shook his head. "I will not add another ghost to that
boy's shoulders. That's the least I can do for him."

*P*EELING HARD WADS OF THE DARK house's soil from
between his toes, Numamushi thought of poison and
the curse Mizukiyo carried.

Father had once bitten open a dead cat to show Numamushi a fire-belly newt in its innards. If the hungry cat, he said, had had the choice of eating a house gecko, it would have been alive. If the cat could have afforded to go hungrier, to choose to eat nothing, it would have been alive too.

"To be able to choose at all is precious and rare, little marshworm. For most, the land doesn't allow any choice but to die for having no choices at all," Father had said, letting the river take the cat away. "I wish those dear to me life—and, for life, to have choices, always."

It didn't sound as if Mizukiyo had been given any choice about his curses and skins at all.

"You've been looking at me more than your calligraphy today." Mizukiyo set down his brush and raised his thin eyebrows. "Do you not like that symbol? Or have I suddenly turned into a frog?"

"When are you going to shed your skin?"

Mizukiyo froze, as he always did when his skin was mentioned. "That's none of your business."

"If you shed your skin, you could meet Father." If the curse for Father was in Mizukiyo's skin, then all Mizukiyo had to do was shed it to be free of it, unless living in the poisonous dark house would only soak the curse back into him. "I could show you good places to shed. I know lots around here!"

"Why do you think I'd want to meet your father?"

"Don't you?"

Mizukiyo came out from behind his desk. His hands opened slowly at his sides, like fangs being bared. "Does he know what he did to me?"

The summer rains rustled outside. The scurrying noise of it was like thousands of insects with their hard, clawed feet and pincering jaws suddenly fleeing the house.

Mizukiyo took off his glasses, folding them as he sat on the floor in front of Numamushi. "Does he know that he made me like this?"

"Like how?"

The shining mirror gleam in Mizukiyo's eyes caught the light, unmistakeable.

For a long time Mizukiyo looked at him. Numamushi stayed still, killing his breath as he had once done in their game in the paddy. He felt that if he moved then, if he so much as blinked or shifted the paper at his fingertips, he would be bitten and eaten whole, snapped up like a frog.

A moment passed, and another, and there were no biting hands, no furious fangs.

Mizukiyo sat back. He covered his face with a hand. "I'm sorry, Numamushi. Please, don't be scared. I won't hurt you. Ah, what am I doing? There's no use getting angry with you. It's not your fault if we're in the same boat."

"Same boat?"

"A boat is a floating leaf big enough that humans can ride on it in water. What I mean to say is..." Mizukiyo gathered himself together and said, slowly, "...I know you're my brother, Numamushi."

"Brother?"

"Yes. Kin. Born of the same house. Or I suppose river."

Numamushi sat up straight. "Your brother?"

"Yes, Numamushi. You're my one and only little brother, whether by birth or adoption or some strange spell of his, I don't know, but you are what you are, and I am what I am."

"We're brothers!"

"Whether you like it or not."

"But I want to be brothers!" Numamushi's heart was full and warm. He didn't understand how Mizukiyo could look so small sitting in front of him, coiled up tight and fearful, as if Numamushi would bite him for saying such a wonderful thing. "Why wouldn't I want us to be brothers?"

"Most wouldn't."

"Why?"

"I've a way with words, Numamushi." Mizukiyo was tentative, like meltwater seeping out of cracked ice. "I was taught to use words carefully and healingly, to make medicine of them as often as I could. But instead..."

"Instead?"

"...never mind. I'd be lying if I said that if I'd met you sooner, I would've been a better man with my words. Words are water, little one. Remember that. Now." Mizukiyo took up Numamushi's blank leaf. "What's going on here? Usually you're so keen to draw I have to stop you wasting paper. You don't like this one?"

"You said it was a double-headed snake, killing a river." Numamushi scowled at the example Mizukiyo had left him to copy. "One head at the source, the other at the end, drinking it to nothing."

"A double-headed dragon, yes. That's one theory for how this symbol was developed. I thought you'd appreciate it."

虹

It was the symbol for a rainbow, the colored band in the sky that Numamushi had always thought of as a bridge much like the one he and Father lived beneath. The left half was the insect symbol that had once read *snake*, the second symbol of Numamushi's name. The right half painted this snake's specific double-headed shape, the arcing body of the dragon as it drank a river dry.

Numamushi shook his head. "It's scary. It could kill Father."

"Hm, you're right. In hindsight, I didn't think this one through." Mizukiyo ran a hand through his own hair. The skin at his hairline creased, stiff in a way that Numamushi recognized: dead skin, with new creeping in beneath. His shedding should be soon. "Let's stop for today. Let's play a game."

"A game! Outside?"

"No, not outside, it's raining."

"So?"

"That means I'm in a mood to stay indoors until it clears. Let's give the frogs a holiday from terror. How about I teach you cards? There's a tin of peaches if you win."

"When I win."

"Oh, the arrogance of the young and ignorant." Mizukiyo ruffled Numamushi's hair, combing it out of his eyes. "We'll see about that, little brother."

Little brother.

Numamushi liked the sound of that. He happily helped Mizukiyo clear away their brushes, ink trays, and drawings of river-killers.

*W*HEN THE RAIN ENDED, the sun was setting. The land glistened with the red-gold glinting fire of dragonfly wings.

Numamushi was hungry. In a fit of pride, he had turned down Mizukiyo's offer to catch them both frogs for dinner. He could catch his own food, thank you, and wasn't to be babied. And so, tired and head-aching from tracing symbols and following the rules of Mizukiyo's card game, he left the dark house to do just that.

Too tired to hunt, he went to the storehouse four paddies downriver. That day there were three mice on the stripe of tape on the floor, squealing and stuck fast, the perfect meal. Numamushi swallowed two, then charmed the last and stuffed it down the front of his clothes.

Father was waiting for him beneath the bridge, flicking his white tongue in the foam of the rain-swollen river. As soon as Numamushi stepped into the water, he curled around him.

"I had a thought today," said Father, "that I would lose you, and that all my power in this land wouldn't be enough to keep you with me."

Before, Numamushi would have said that there was nothing in the land more powerful than Father, but in that moment, the double-headed snake of Mizukiyo's rainbow drew an arc across his mind.

Suddenly feeling cold and more tired than usual, Numamushi clung to Father's scales and shivered. Tomorrow he would defeat the rainbow. He would draw it as many times as it took until the symbol could be scribbled small and fast, and it looked less like a double-headed river-killer and more like a scattering of slugs and eels.

Until the river-killer could be killed.

"NUMAMUSHI, NUMAMUSHI, my little one, wake up, wake up, please."

He woke to the smell of blood.

"Please, my dear, you have to tell me—where did you go today? What did you eat?" A gentle shake, then a shake that was less gentle. "Please, little marshworm, you must tell me! Was it him? Did that boy give you something?"

The water weighed on Numamushi's limbs. He tried to breathe. His throat was too small.

"My dear, please." The white snake's tongue swept over him, kissing his forehead clean, stirring the blood in the water to a dark smoke. "Speak, tell me, or else I'm lost for how to save you."

"Not Mizukiyo." Blood was floating from Numamushi's nose in bubbles, catching the light reflecting from Father's mirror eyes, the pearl of his scales. Blood was running from Numamushi's gums too. It slid between his teeth. "This..." He found the mouse in his robes, its back bald where he'd peeled it from the storehouse tape. "This, Father."

Father touched his tongue to it. "This?!"

Numamushi wanted to nod, but his head was too heavy and the water was spinning. When he closed his eyes, black slugs and eels swam behind them. All about him Father slithered, swayed, his coils rocking Numamushi in their cradle. He was talking to him, pleading, but his words fell against Numamushi's ears like foam and Numamushi couldn't reply. Blood filled his nose, flowed back into his mouth. He was wading somewhere within himself, through clinging mud that was soft and dragging. He'd been named for the marsh, for its murky safety and the soothing touch of its water. He wasn't lost here, so why was Father calling his name?

"I'm not lost, Father," he murmured, as the coils around him shifted, their shape changing with clicks and cracks of bone but still holding him firmly, tightly, as if Numamushi would slip away with the river's current. "You don't need to call my name."

"I know, Numamushi. I know you're not lost, you won't be."

It struck Numamushi that he was no longer being held in coils but in arms—long, human arms with thin-fingered hands, bundled in the folds of robes as white as moonlight—and that it wasn't the river current buffeting his face but the wind, wet from the day's rain. It wasn't bubbles in his ears but frog song, rising loud and clear with night. He coughed and sneezed, and his blood didn't curl away in a cloud but splattered over white cloth with a silver embroidery of scales, as Father ran, fast as the river at its angriest and fullest, ran up over the bank and in great gliding steps over the paddy, begging for Numamushi to stay and hold on, and whispering his name, over and over again.

Why, Father? He wanted to open his mouth to say it, but his mouth would do nothing but push out the bloodied spit pooling under his tongue. *Why are you calling me? I'm not lost, I'm right here...*

The haze of the dark marsh was warm, soft, and safe behind his eyes, and Numamushi felt no need to open them—not until Father came to an abrupt stop, arms quivering and chest rising and falling quickly.

The dark house's allotment was at Father's feet.

"Mizukiyo!" The water of his voice crashed against the dark house and broke. It wasn't loud, but it had the river's land-carving, rock-splitting power. Numamushi curled his fingers into Father's robes, urging him not to hurt or harm, because it wasn't Mizukiyo's fault. "Mizukiyo, help him!"

There was no answer, no movement from the house. Father hesitated no more. He stepped onto the dark house's land and kept running, up the steps to the yard, past the dark, crooked line of the persimmon tree. "Mizukiyo!"

A light appeared, an orange zinnia, then the square of an open veranda door.

Numamushi blinked. He saw two Mizukiyos: one on the veranda, a dark silhouette with the mirror gleam of his eyes burning; the other, face framed in white hair that trailed long over Numamushi's body, holding Numamushi so closely the thud of his heart made the slugs in Numamushi's head sway.

"Help him," said the one who held Numamushi, white

tongue flashing between teeth. "He's eaten poison. Please, Mizukiyo, I beg you. Help him."

"He always speaks of you as if you know everything and have the power to do anything," said the mirror-eyed shadow. "Why can't you help him?"

"This isn't within my power. This is a human-made poison. Nothing I know of this land or its water will save him. He needs human help." He held Numamushi out to the one on the veranda. "He calls you brother."

"And what do you call me?"

The wind rustled over the dark house's poisoned land. Whatever Father said, Numamushi didn't hear it.

Crawling filled his ears, a slippery-sliding rush of dark things twisting and writhing in soil. The darkness of the house shrilled, howled, hummed of emptiness and the ghosts of wasps. It snapped with the burred tongue of the wind blowing through hollowed eaves where the nests had hung, fat as moons, now gone. It stretched toward Father as a hungry shadow. It swallowed moonlight, devoured the light of Father's scales, turned the glow of white hair to streaming foam that broke on the backs of dark waves.

Red zinnias blossomed, unfurling bright on white.

He couldn't stay awake, not even with the smell and taste of blood bursting sharp as berries in his nose and mouth. With zinnias in his eyes, Numamushi closed them.

He felt a pair of hands as he slipped into the marsh of his mind, prying him from Father's gentle teeth and lifting him away.

"AFTER YOU'VE REGISTERED him at the municipal office, let me know how he is. My surgery's just around the corner from it."

"I shall. Thank you, doctor, and..."

A rustle of paper.

"Oh, I couldn't possibly—"

"For coming out at this hour." Another rustle. "And as an expression of my gratitude and respect for the professional discretion I know you'll show."

"Ah. I see. Yes, indeed. I understand." The front door opened; Numamushi knew its sound by the rattle of the metal frame in the rut. "You're lucky it's that new-fangled warfarin stuff. If it was the old phosphorus or arsenic rat poisons, I doubt even that child's...natural robustness could have saved him."

"Thank you, doctor. Good night."

The front door closed.

A tall shadow returned from the porch, steps quiet and hurried.

Numamushi breathed. "Who...?"

"Hush now." Mirror eyes caught the glow of a candle set in a paper lantern. "Go to sleep, Numamushi. You don't want to be awake yet."

The shadow's words soothed, curled, cradled. Numamushi let the charm in the voice sink him beneath the warm and quiet silt of his thoughts.

IN NUMAMUSHI'S DREAMS HE HAD BEEN trapped in weeds and long white hair.

Reality was a thin blanket, damp with sweat. He was lying on a long pad, flat and defenseless on his back—a position he had never before slept in—and tangled in the covers.

Smoke rose from a mosquito coil burning in a tin by the veranda door. Mizukiyo sat beside him, the split bamboo frame of his fan creaking softly as he wafted cool air over them both.

"Mizu..."

Mizukiyo stopped fanning. He sat forwards quickly. "Are you trying to say my name? Or do you want water?"

Everything in Numamushi's mouth tasted of old blood. "Water."

"Yes, of course. Wait here. Don't get up. I'll charm you if I have to."

"Not a frog. Don't charm me."

A strained laugh. Mizukiyo went.

Numamushi looked around the room. The floor was the same wheat-scented tatami he'd learned to scrub the ink from in the classroom. In one corner was a paper lantern with white windows and a black frame. In the other corner were a small chest of drawers and a low desk with calligraphy paper. The walls of the room were panelled, each with a handle, each a door. They'd been painted with scenes of people and animals, with lonely clouds and windswept trees.

"Here." Mizukiyo returned with a cup in hand. He held it out to Numamushi, who sat up gingerly to take it. Mizukiyo's glasses were gone, set aside on the desk. "How are you feeling?"

"Hungry." Numamushi sniffed, then wrinkled his nose.

He smelled as if he hadn't been in the river in days. "And too dry. My elbows are flaky."

Mizukiyo took the empty cup from his hand. "Living out of the river, you'll have to get used to that."

Something in his tone made Numamushi look up. Suddenly he didn't see this Mizukiyo but the other, the white-faced one with white hair, white tongue between their teeth, who had carried him to the dark house.

Father. That had been Father. Father had carried him from their river, pressing him into Mizukiyo's care, asking for a human to help put out the poison burning in Numamushi's blood—except that couldn't have been Father, because Father had said that if he went to the dark house, if he met Mizukiyo—

Mizukiyo's hand settled on Numamushi's head, combed the hair out of his eyes. "Father's gone, Numamushi."

"Gone where?" His own voice sounded like a small thing, huddled in the grass.

"Perhaps...China?"

"China?" That was the land where Mizukiyo's symbols came from. "Why would Father go there?"

"Perhaps because it's faraway place and he's decided to go on a long journey."

"I'm six summers old, Mizukiyo, I'm not small!" The words flew from Numamushi, sharp and biting, and he knew they'd bitten when Mizukiyo flinched. "I can catch my own food! I know how to kill and eat! I know things!"

"Things?" Mizukiyo said softly. "Like what, Numamushi?"

Numamushi bunched his hands. He was clutching his covers like he had clutched Father's moon-white robes. They had slithered smooth in his grip, like snakeskin. He should have held on tighter. He should have weighed heavy on Father's collar and dragged him back to the hollow under the bridge, rather than let him go to the poisoned land! To look into Mizukiyo's poisonous face! To accept the curse from his skin!

"I know what happened." His eyes burned. Something wet slithered down his face and his cheek shuddered beneath it. "I know there was a curse waiting here for Father...in the land, and in..."

Your skin, Numamushi didn't say. Mizukiyo was trying so hard to be kind, to bundle everything up in the gentle water of his words. He'd never had a choice with his curse. Numamushi had stolen that choice from him when he'd picked those mice from the tape and sent Father running to the only human who could save him.

"Mizukiyo—"

"Numamushi—"

Mizukiyo cleared his throat. "You can go first."

I'm sorry should have been on the tip of Numamushi's tongue, but when he spoke, the words became altogether different.

"I wish you hadn't come here."

Mizukiyo said nothing. Numamushi closed his eyes and willed himself to cry. He wanted those tears that Father had spoken about, to cool the hurt burning in his chest and wash it all away.

Maybe Numamushi wasn't human enough to cry properly, for all that he had a name. Maybe tears wouldn't work for him at all, with his flaky elbows, the mice in his guts, and his silver-white snakeskin robes. They were racing cold and slippery as tadpoles down his face to his collar, but the hurt wasn't leaving him. If anything, he felt as if he was slipping deeper into it like a current. Father had never told him that pain had its own undertow.

Arms wrapped tightly around Numamushi and pulled him close.

"If I'd known you were here, I would never have come." Mizukiyo sighed into the top of Numamushi's head. "I don't know what I'm doing anymore. Ah, little one. You've made things difficult for me. I'm so sorry."

If Numamushi closed his eyes and only listened, this could have been Father, wrapping him in his scaly coils, keeping him safe, holding him back from being swept away by dangerous waters.

But it wasn't, and because it wasn't and never would be again, he hurt, and wept, and still hurt.

Water landed on his forehead. Mizukiyo's mirror eyes wept with him.

THE RIVER CHANGED after Father died. It wasn't Father's river anymore. His power over the land vanished, and the water ran as it wished.

Numamushi had no desire to return to the river, not when all it promised was emptiness. He stayed in the dark house, first one night, then another, going out during the day to search for a drain or hollow that he liked enough to make his own, until on the third night he realized that Mizukiyo didn't expect him to leave the dark house at all.

He got his own padded mat and his own blanket to put down every night. It was strange at first to have to lie, belly up, on a surface that was so still and flat. The first night, he huddled against Mizukiyo's back, just so that he wasn't surrounded by the lonely stillness of the gaping air and hard floor. The second night, Mizukiyo quietly pushed him away, telling him it was too hot to be sleeping back to back, and Numamushi had had to agree that this was true. Summer out of the water was truly unbearable.

But they remained in the same room, laying their mats side by side against the heavy darkness of the nighttime house.

Clothes were next. Pale shirts with folded collars, grey shorts, and hitoe were delivered from the village, and went straight into a space behind one of the doors in the wall. This door was for a "closet."

"It's a hole for hiding whatever you want."

"Can I keep frogs there?" Numamushi asked eagerly, exploring the closet's narrow space.

"No more than five at a time and only if they're charmed."

Charmed frogs weren't any fun, but the cotton clothes Mizukiyo had given Numamushi didn't stay clean like Father's skin did, so he supposed it would save on washing. In his closet, he put his best symbol drawings, his clothes and linens, and, in an empty peach tin, cicada husks and bean pods and whatever else he collected from outside.

The rest of the sleeping room's closets belonged to Mizu-kiyo. Numamushi approached the closet closest to the door, the one painted with a pair of figures.

Mizukiyo grabbed his wrist. "Don't open that one."

"Why not?"

"Because I may hurt you if you do, even if I don't want to." The jaw of Mizukiyo's hand was strong, its grip on Numamushi just short of painful. "I can't count on being able to help myself. I've failed every time before."

The itching in Numamushi's fingers to pry immedi-ately faded. He'd already stolen one choice from Mizukiyo. Numamushi lowered his hand and promised himself that he would never touch this closet, not unless Mizukiyo chose to let him.

The people painted on Mizukiyo's closet wore robes with trailing green and white sleeves. Now that Numamushi was closer, he could see how their bodies turned long and pale and tapered to coiling points.

"Who are they?"

"Those are Fu Hsi and Nuwa." Sensing Numamushi's shift of interest, Mizukiyo let him go. "In one of China's stories, these two half-snake gods created the first humans from mud and ropes. All over the world, Numamushi, snakes have been seen as the most divine of creatures. It was the snake that ate the god's fruit in the Epic of Gilgamesh, and the snake that nightly devoured Egypt's sun god, and the snake Python that was the oracle, the mouth of the old gods of Greece. You find snakes beside gods everywhere, their equals if not gods them-selves. Immortal, you see, so divine for it."

"Immortal?"

"People thought that shedding their skin meant snakes never aged and never died. That is 'immortal.' Then they could become very old and know many things."

"Like Father?"

"Yes. Like Father." Then the same hand as had been holding Numamushi back from the closet went to his hair, ruffling it guiltily. "One theory for the origins of our word for snake, *hebi*, is that it comes from *henmi*, or *those of changing bodies*. We shed our skins, so we can change. Be reborn. Say goodbye to ourselves over and over again." He fell silent, his hand still resting in Numamushi's hair, then laughed strangely. "But another theory is that *hebi* comes from *hamu—to eat*. 'Insatiable eating machine.' So, true to our heritage, let's make lunch."

It was a day without calligraphy classes. Mizukiyo allowed Numamushi to bring a pot of frogs into the dark house and release them into the corridors, so Numamushi put the closet with the divine snake-people quickly out of his mind.

That night, in his dream, the slugs and eels of Mizukiyo's symbols ran in an ink-dark river from a mountain—in China, Numamushi guessed. That was where Mizukiyo said the letters came from: a spring full of eels in China, becoming a river that flowed into and through Father's land, becoming Father, black ink bubbling with white scales.

"Father!" Numamushi called.

But, of course, the white snake had had no name. There was no calling him back. Wherever he had gone to, Father would not have strayed. Snakes and rivers were never lost.

*H*UMANS WERE A DIFFERENT MATTER. Humans liked names, more than Numamushi had expected.

Mizukiyo presented Numamushi one morning with a series of symbols on a sheet of paper.

"In case we have visitors, I want you to learn this." He tapped each symbol, one by one, as he read them off. "*Mizobata Jasuke*. Now, your turn."

"*Mizobata Jasuke*. What does that mean?"

"It's your name. Your official name," Mizukiyo amended when Numamushi hissed with confusion. "It's the one I put down to make you a part of human society. *Mizobata*: you share this with me. It means that if someone hurts you, they hurt me too, so I can bite them back for it. *Jasuke* is for you. If someone comes looking for the Mizobatas, but they want you, not me, this is what they'll call you by."

Numamushi considered the symbols Mizukiyo had given him. These were his. He took the paper to hoard in his closet but also asked, "What's wrong with Numamushi?"

"It's not a name people would expect my little brother to be called by."

"So?"

"It helps to have at least one name that fits with people's expectations. Other people, who aren't your family or friends, might need it to call you."

"Why would other people need to call me anything?"

"They can see you now, can't they?" Numamushi nodded. His ability to go by unseen to humans hadn't disappeared entirely, but it was weaker since Father had gone. Numamushi had to work harder to hide himself with his own power now.

53

"Then, just in case, I'm giving you this name."

"In case of what?"

"Well, if something happens to me—"

"It won't."

"Now, Numamushi—"

"I said it won't. You're not going anywhere."

"This name will protect you when you're seen by others," Mizukiyo said without raising his voice, but the mirror gleam in his eyes brightened in a way that made Numamushi want to find a stone and hide beneath it, "so when we have visitors and my students come round—"

"What students?" Because for all the days Numamushi had been there, not a single calligraphy student had come by the house.

"—when my students come round," Mizukiyo jabbed the paper with every word he spoke, "I will be calling you Jasuke, and they will know by this name that you are protected by me, and, if they are good humans, that you should be protected by them too."

"That's not fair."

"What have names to do with fairness?"

Numamushi folded his arms. "What do I call you when your students come round? How do I protect *you* with a name?"

"You can call me..." Mizukiyo seemed taken aback. If Numamushi didn't know better, he'd think he was nervous, even scared, "...*Niisan*, if you wish."

Big brother. "Will that protect you?"

"It might. In a fashion. Though I wouldn't deserve it."

Numamushi peered into Mizukiyo's face. Then he pushed a sheet of blank paper towards him. "Write it down. I want to learn what that word looks like too. *Niisan*."

*M*IZUKIYO'S SKIN had been dull and dry even before Numamushi moved into the dark house. It should've been shed not long after Numamushi shed his own skin, and yet Mizukiyo hadn't even peeled off a toe.

Every night, Numamushi woke to the air slithering, thick and humid, into their room. Each time Mizukiyo would be out of bed, gazing out of the open veranda door to the river, scratching and pinching his arms. Numamushi recognized that restlessness from when his own skin was overdue. It was the body's way of saying that it was going to be soft and new soon. It needed to find somewhere safe enough for that to happen.

But when Numamushi told Mizukiyo that he should find a nice ditch, somewhere darker and damper than the dusty, dark house, and that he shouldn't need to be shy about shedding in front of his students—if that was what was holding him back—Mizukiyo laughed and set Numamushi to helping him clean the house, as if in petty vengeance.

It was as if Mizukiyo was determined to pretend his skin wasn't shedding. Or he was refusing to shed altogether.

Why? What good would that do? It would only make Mizukiyo sick and miserable. Why would he wish to go around bundled in dead skin like a dry and prickly robe?

As Numamushi was sweeping the hall, pondering this, the front door flew open with a clatter.

"Kiyo! Are you there? Hello? Oh!" Spotting Numamushi with his broom, Tora paused in taking off his shoes. "Who's this? Kiyo, you got yourself a disciple already? Hello, kid! Don't look so scared! Here." Tora patted his bulging coat pockets. "I've got some fruity *ame-chan* from the city on me somewhere. Aha! There we go. Go on, kid. It's not poison. I'm not out to kill the future of the nation. Ah! Kiyo, there you are!"

"Tora." Mizukiyo came to a stop behind Numamushi. "What are you doing here?"

Tora put his hands on his hips. "I've lost my job!"

"And what has that got to do with me?"

The man grinned. "Nothing."

"Nothing. I see. And would that 'nothing' explain why you're standing in my entranceway with a lifetime's possessions' worth of luggage?"

Tora had a large sack slung over each shoulder, a briefcase in one hand, and two small pouches belted to each leg. Despite the summer heat, he wore three coats, two hats, and a scarf. Shoes were stuffed down his front.

Sweat dribbled from his hairline. Tora smiled weakly. "A cup of tea before I faint?"

Mizukiyo sighed. "Come in, you idiot."

Tora didn't hide his curiosity. He stared openly as Numamushi brought tea to the classroom where he and Mizukiyo sat. Numamushi had to suppress a shiver at the still-strange sensation of being seen.

"Thank you, kid." The tea went from the tray straight to Tora's mouth. He swallowed and smacked his lips. "Ah! I am reborn! Now, what's your name and how'd you come to be student to this snake here?"

"Jasuke is my little brother," said Mizukiyo, indicating for Numamushi to sit on the cushion beside him.

"Little brother!? Since when?"

"Believe me, it was as much as a surprise to me as it is to you." Mizukiyo refilled all their cups. "Our father turned up and left him here with me. He didn't leave either Jasuke or me much choice."

Tora looked up from his cup. "You met your father?"

"Yes."

"He was alive all along?" Tora snorted when Mizukiyo swept a hand towards Numamushi, as though Numamushi was proof of that. Numamushi didn't understand, but he stayed coiled on his cushion and studied Tora in case he needed biting. "Where's your old man gone then?"

"I don't know."

"Really? What happened to looking your father in the eye, having him know your name and face, and giving him a piece of your mind?"

"And it doesn't matter." Mizukiyo picked up his glasses from the table and settled them on his nose. "Wherever he went, he's never coming back."

"Did you at least get a chance to talk to him?"

"We talked."

"And?"

"He was better than I deserved to meet."

Tora sat back. He looked between Mizukiyo and Numamushi. He nodded approvingly. "You look like each other."

Numamushi blinked at Mizukiyo, surprised and delighted. "Really?"

"Sure, you do, kid!" Tora beamed. "You've got the same angry eyebrows, like you'd both bite me if I put a foot wrong."

"I would," Numamushi agreed.

Tora laughed and reached out to pat or pinch him. Numamushi didn't wait to find out which; he dodged with a hiss. "Aw, Jasuke, our little Jasuke. How do you write your name?"

"With *ja* for snake." Mizukiyo watched the two of them over the brim of his cup.

"Let the boy talk for himself! I bet your horrible big brother's tried drumming all his favorite horrible symbols into you. He has, hasn't he? This calligraphy obsessive."

"Niisan isn't horrible."

"It's all right, kid. You can be honest with me. From now on, if this one makes you cry," Tora pointed at Mizukiyo, who raised his eyebrows, "you can come and tell me all about it. I had seven little brothers before the war. Little Tatsuo, he was about your age when I saw him last. You can tell me anything. I'm the big brother of big brothers." He winked, then tipped his head at Mizukiyo and whispered conspiratorially, "We'll look out for this one together, eh? Stop him slithering off into the shadows on his own?"

"Tora." Mizukiyo's voice cut coolly between them. "Why does it sound as if you're here to stay?"

Tora set down his cup. Numamushi saw the clench of his hands on his knees. "Would you turn me away if I was?"

Mizukiyo should. Mizukiyo wasn't shedding his skin. Father would have said that he needed peace and quiet. That he wouldn't have time to spare for another mouth in their home.

But perhaps...if Mizukiyo was already ill, in some way that stopped him from shedding, it wouldn't be bad to have someone else in the house to look after him—just as Tora had said.

In the end, Numamushi said nothing, because this was Mizukiyo's choice. Tora was Mizukiyo's "friend" and "family."

Mizukiyo said, "Tell me exactly how you lost your job, Tora."

NUMAMUSHI DIDN'T UNDERSTAND most of Tora's story. He didn't know what journalists were, although he'd once found a newspaper sheet wrapped around a small harvest of beans and taken it to Father out of curiosity. He didn't know what *Japan* was, either. The words *General MacArthur* and *Prime Minister Yoshida* bumped against his ears and then buzzed on, alongside phrases so strange that he couldn't tell if they were people or places, like *Red Purge* and *last year's National Railway Mysteries*.

What he did understand was that they all meant things to Mizukiyo, things that made his jaw tighten to bite—and that had taken away the work by which Tora kept his house.

"I should've stayed going door-to-door, selling vinyl raincoats or something. Sales and advertising!" Tora had brought food in his bags. He cracked eggs, one after the other, into a small pan. Numamushi watched from his elbow, fascinated as clear egg juices sputtered, then turned white and fleshy and thick. "The only places where the power of words remains! And they won't take the power from them because that power nudges along the economy! But journalism? Academia? No more words for us. No. More. Words."

"Words are water, Tora," said Mizukiyo, from where he was airing the steamed rice. It sounded to Numamushi like a warning.

"So you always say, so you always say," Tora replied airily, before glancing over at Mizukiyo and laughing. "Here, Kiyo, don't squash the rice like that. You want to fluff it, like blankets. Don't you cook anymore since moving into this haunted palace?"

Not lately, when the rains had been bringing the frogs out. Mizukiyo and Numamushi had been eating their fill from the paddies each day. Before going to the kitchen, Numamushi had asked Mizukiyo if they needed to go hunting for more frogs, extra for Tora, but Mizukiyo had shaken his head. More worryingly, he'd made Numamushi promise not to speak of eating frogs in front of him.

"Why not?"

"It'd make him..." Mizukiyo had searched for a word, which was unlike him as well. "...ill. Anything about catching and eating animals live will make him ill. Then angry. With me, more than you. So don't speak of it in front of him. Or eat them in front of him. Do you understand?"

"No food in the house?"

"That's right." Mizukiyo had looked sad then, the mirror in his eyes tired. "No food in the house. Oh, and say nothing about skin, or shedding it, either."

"But—"

"Tora is a good man, but even he has limits." Mizukiyo had crouched to Numamushi's height, urging him to listen. "I don't want to learn what they are."

There was real fear in Mizukiyo's eyes. The thought of what could make Mizukiyo afraid made Numamushi afraid too. He nodded, if reluctantly.

"How long is he going to stay here?" Numamushi asked.

Mizukiyo shook his head. He didn't know. Numamushi did his best to bury all thoughts of skin, however urgent, in the marsh at the back of his mind.

Tora went to bring in his bags from the porch, humming and singing fragments of tunes he claimed were "popular in the city," that "everyone but cursed calligraphy teachers" knew.

IF MIZUKIYO'S VOICE was the river, Tora's was the mountain. When he talked—which was constantly—his words were firm and sunlit, cutting solidly through haze and rain. Numamushi ended up smiling even as Tora teased him or the man sang rowdily in the bath.

He liked Tora. He liked listening to Tora. He liked listening to Mizukiyo and Tora talking together, even though a lot of what they said might as well have been slugs and eels in his ears. Best of all, Tora made Mizukiyo smile, more often and warmly than Numamushi had seen yet.

For instance, on his first night, Tora had picked up his bedding from where Mizukiyo had laid it in the room by the porch and dragged it to join Mizukiyo and Numamushi in their room.

"Please, Kiyo."

"No, you oaf. I remember how you snored in Burma."

"Please?" Tora had pleaded, clutching his mat. "You know I don't like ghosts. I am not sleeping on my own in your haunted murder-house."

"You've slept fine in a haunted jungle surrounded by ghosts who'd actually have good reason to want you dead."

"Jasuke!" Tora had appealed this time to Numamushi. "Tell your cold-hearted Kiyo-nii that Tora-nii is a coward and a crybaby and that if he makes Tora sleep on his own in this murder-house, he will wet the tatami."

And Mizukiyo had relented, not with a sigh, but with a smile.

With Tora in the room, Mizukiyo had slept soundly all night without once getting up, even though Tora snored like a choir of frogs lived in his throat. Numamushi too, with Mizukiyo on one side of him and Tora on the other, felt, for the first time since leaving the river, as safe and surrounded as he had with Father in the hollow.

Tora stayed one night, and then another, and another. During the days he went out to "jobseek." He came back in the evenings, soaked in rain and with his feet muddy, teeth clenched in a frustrated grimace, which always became the broadest of smiles when Numamushi or Mizukiyo met him at the door.

Perhaps, Tora could make Mizukiyo feel safe enough to shed his skin.

If that was so, Numamushi decided that Tora could stay as long as he liked.

"HOW LONG do I intend to stay?" Tora thought for a moment, then went back to weeding the allotment. "Only as long as you and Mizukiyo let me. Don't worry, Jasuke, I'm working on finding myself what gainful employment I can—where my words won't hurt no-one. By the way, I couldn't help noticing, when I gave you that newspaper this morning. You can't read. Right?"

"I can too read!"

"I'm not saying you weren't trying. Your eyes were moving the wrong way, that's all. You're seeing the symbols, but you aren't joining them together. Right?" At Numamushi's scowl, Tora shook his hoe. "Man's got to be able to read and write, Jasuke, or he's a slave forever to everyone who can. You could end up delivering your own death sentence to your executioner and you wouldn't be able to tell that memo apart from an ant trail. What say I teach you?"

Numamushi paused, hands on the washing line. He had been offered something, and his instincts told him it was a frog, but he didn't want to jump at frogs anymore. If something looked too easily offered, he could end up poisoned and bleeding again, and who would he lose this time?

He thought of words and of being able to make them flow together on paper like Mizukiyo's voice did in the air, because that was what the newspaper had looked like when he'd opened it that morning—a rushing torrent of words. It had made him think of his dream of a river of ink.

He decided. "You can teach me."

"Really?"

"Yes."

"Well, damn! Great! Brilliant! You're a good kid, Jasuke." Tora reached out to ruffle Numamushi's hair just like Mizukiyo did, but when his hand drew too close, Numamushi couldn't help himself. He ducked and snapped.

He'd bitten into the soft meat between Tora's thumb and forefinger before he even realized his mouth was opening.

Numamushi froze. He looked up. Tora's eyes were wide and white, but before Numamushi could let go to run and hide in the paddy or in his closet, Tora threw back his head and laughed long and hard.

"You're just like your brother! He bit me when I first tried to touch his hair too! Kiyo! Kiyo!" Before Numamushi could stop him, Tora had pulled free from his teeth and run delightedly back to the house, holding up his bleeding hand like a prize. "Your little brother bit me! We're definitely friends now!"

The blood drained from Mizukiyo's face. "Let me see that!"

"Hey, don't worry. It's a baby bite. It won't even scar. Unlike with you."

"Jasuke!"

"Kiyo, I startled him, he didn't mean any harm. Besides, it's not like he's venomous or anything...What's so funny?"

"Nothing." Mizukiyo bit off an ugly, low-pitched laugh. "You're right, that's all. But I'm not letting him off. Jasuke!"

Mizukiyo set Numamushi to weeding the allotment in Tora's stead. Numamushi didn't argue. Father wouldn't have been happy with Numamushi either and, more crushingly, Numamushi was disappointed in himself. He wasn't so small anymore that he thought with his teeth first and head later. He took the hoe and gloves from Tora, watched Mizukiyo lead Tora into the house to clean the bite, then got to work.

Striped mosquitoes whined against his face. They made Numamushi long for the dark shadow of the bridge and the balmy coolness of the river. Luckily, they'd never much liked to bite him.

The sun reached its peak. Mizukiyo must have been more upset with Numamushi than he'd thought, as nobody came out to fetch him for lunch. Numamushi's stomach began to turn his nose towards the paddy, and nudge, and gnaw, and worry, with every irregular rustle of movement in the rice.

It wouldn't hurt, surely, to catch just one small frog. Or even a diving beetle. Just to distract his belly until Mizukiyo's anger passed over.

There was no sign of anyone coming from the house. Numamushi set down the hoe, folded up his clothes as Mizukiyo had shown him, and slipped into the paddy.

Ten rounds of ten heartbeats later, he surfaced, frog caught happily between his teeth. He pulled himself onto the paddy wall, knocked the water out of his ears, and was busy shaking it from his hair when he felt eyes on him.

Too late, Numamushi remembered that his ability to go unseen wasn't what it used to be.

Tora was standing a short distance away on the wall, staring, seeing, his mouth agape.

Numamushi froze, stuck for what to do, a half-eaten frog's legs hanging from his mouth. He waited for Tora to make a move.

Tora took a towel from the laundry pole and held it out to him.

"I've eaten people, Jasuke," he said. "And the maggots that were on them. Raw and fried. I'm not going to judge you, when I'm never going to eat prawn sashimi again for the rest of my life."

Prawn? Maggots? What was he talking about?

"Come on, kid. Your horrible brother sent me to fetch you in. Let's get you dry—and look how tidy you've made this sorry patch of land! You're a champion weeder!"

And that was it. Tora was still smiling, still laughing, even as Numamushi sucked up the rest of the frog and swallowed it. He helped Numamushi wash and dry before going into the house. He said not a word to Mizukiyo that he'd caught Numamushi hunting in the paddy, and made them all lunch.

Tora wasn't ill or angry. He talked loudly about the old men he'd found for Mizukiyo's calligraphy classes. They had come to the house not long after Numamushi had been put to punishment in the allotment. Suddenly occupied with these students, Tora and Mizukiyo hadn't been able to bring in Numamushi until they were gone.

Numamushi could have become jealous when Tora chattered of finding more students, perhaps at the "local middle school," but all he felt was a slug of worry. Mizukiyo still hadn't shed his skin. He was eating less, putting his rice gruel in Numamushi's bowl when he thought Tora wasn't looking, and he was reluctant, afraid even, to catch food with Tora in the house.

Perhaps Mizukiyo needed to hear that Tora didn't seem to mind it, that there was nothing to be afraid of, but then Numamushi would have to admit that Tora had spotted him hunting, and he had scared Mizukiyo once that day already.

IZUKIYO AND TORA were still in the classroom, talking in low voices, when Numamushi finished cleaning the bath.

"School won't be kind to him."

"Life won't be kind to him, Kiyo. Not if you don't let him get even the most basic education. What's he going to do if you suddenly have to leave him on his own?"

"That won't happen."

"Can you guarantee that? You've seen the papers. Korea, and all. Who's to say you're not going to be conscripted by the next winter, for someone's war, somewhere? This time next year, we could be laying tracks in Siberia until our backs break or half-dead of the jungle runnies, praying that we could be more than half."

"Should it come to that, I've made arrangements. He's in my will. If people are good and can find it within themselves to do as they should, then it should be good enough."

"'If people are good.' You don't half ask much of people." Rain drummed down on the tiles and washed through the gutters. "You know, sometimes, Kiyo, I look at you and I feel like…"

"Like what?"

"Like I'm looking at water. Like you'd flow away if Jasuke wasn't here, forcing you to live like a human."

"Instead of an animal?"

"Or a ghost. Haunting this place. Cursing yourself to never move on."

There was a pause too tangled for Numamushi to break into, so he stayed in the corridor, listening.

"What's this got to do with teaching Jasuke to read and write?"

"Just let me do it. I don't understand why you're so against it. He's a smart kid. I'm not out to humiliate him or make him feel society-dumb."

"Because words are water, Tora."

"That again!"

"And you said that we're alike. Jasuke and I." Mizukiyo lowered his voice further. "He bit you today."

"Well, you did once."

"Exactly, and he shouldn't be like me. He mustn't be like me! I'm almost certain he isn't, but I'm afraid for him if he is!" An almost-whisper: "I want to spare him finding out."

"Finding out that he's like you?" A pause just long enough for a nod. "If he was, what's so terrible about it?"

"When words come out of my mouth, sometimes they're poisonous."

"And sometimes they've saved us!" Numamushi was startled by Tora's fierceness. "They've saved me! In that jungle, when we were starving and we were talking about whether to eat the ones who'd died or not, you told us what we needed to hear to live. You told us that it was still worth living, even when we were putting unspeakable things into our mouths. That we weren't damned just for desperately doing our animal best to escape death and live long enough to come home."

"Yes, we lived," said Mizukiyo faintly, "but I might've sent hundreds and thousands to die. I don't know how many sermons I delivered saying the will of Amida and the will of the Emperor were one and the same, but I used my poison, deliberately, thinking it would make things easier for everyone. I thought I was helping you by easing your minds, but then I was in that prison, talking to all those prisoners, sending them to the gallows, and my words, Tora! My words! I fed them my poison, and all these men who should have been railing to live, kicking and fighting to their very last unsilent second! They all went smiling!" There was a soft thump, like a fist on the floor. "I think of them, Tora. I think of how my poison drove all those people out of their minds, that they could walk into the mouth of death and offer up their necks to it, and I think, what am I that I can do that to them? That I've this poison in my mouth that could make humans die as I asked or wished it? All those people I talked to, whom they let me speak to, I might as well have bitten them like the snake you've always called me."

"I was joking. Don't take that seriously. It was a joke. You're not a snake. You're a good man. The best man I know!"

"What if I really was a snake, Tora?" Something in

Mizukiyo's tone made Numamushi cold all over. "What if I shucked off my skin here and now, turned into some great white monster, and charmed you out of your mind with a look and a bite? To go quietly, smilingly, to your death?"

"You could be Yamata-no-Orochi with eight heads and tails and you'd still be the man who fought and ate and hurt with me in the worst years of my life when I was my own worst self. Not one of us came back from the continent wholly human. If you weren't wholly human to start with, you just had a head start. Since when has 'human' meant much good anyway? It just means 'overthinker.' Which means you're the most human man I know—and with my help reminding you of that, you don't have to worry a thing about what Jasuke learns to do with his words." There was a thick, river-dark pause, like water pooling slow and quiet in the gentle cup of the bridge's hollow. "Ah, Kiyo, you idiot, what's a calligraphy teacher doing being scared of his own words?"

"Calligraphy is safe." Mizukiyo's voice was muffled. "It only asks of words to be beautiful. Alive in their own right. Not to be used."

"All right, all right."

"You think I'm being metaphorical, don't you? About snakes and poison and words."

"You were a priest and a prison chaplain. Speaking in metaphors is a habit you're going to have to break." There was another pause, this time delicate, one that made Numamushi think of a red dragonfly alighting on a stem. "Kiyo, look this way."

"No."

"I wrote a political column. You think I can't handle a poisonous word or two?"

"You can't and I won't, and I can't and you won't."

"You've bitten me once. I survived. Look, scar and all!" Numamushi peered through the gap in the sliding doors. Tora was holding up the other hand, the one Numamushi didn't bite. A pale crescent crawled between thumb and forefinger. "If you were ever poisonous, I'm resistant now."

"It doesn't work like that, you fool."

"Then I was born resistant. You could never hurt me."

"Nothing in the world works like that."

"And you call me the idiot." Tora ran his hand over Mizukiyo's head, down his neck, over his shoulders. He drew Mizukiyo's outlines like the very space he occupied was a hollow Tora could curl into. "You don't need words for this, poisoned or otherwise." That dragonfly lightness alighted again. "Kiyo. Look this way."

Mizukiyo turned. The stem of the moment bent. He pressed his lips to Tora's, gently, carefully, as if to remind Tora of the threat behind his teeth, how easily that seal could slip and break. Tora seemed surprised, but only for an instant. He pressed back, just as gentle, although with a different sort of softness. His was steady, the quiet lift of earth underfoot.

Numamushi looked away, feeling sleepy and soft, like he could lie down in the corridor belly-up and be safe in that moment.

"Jasuke's been a while, hasn't he? Do you think he fell asleep in the bath?"

Numamushi had just enough time to burrow under the covers before Tora opened the door a quiet inch. "Jasuke? Are you asleep?"

Numamushi let his mouth hang open and pretended he was dead.

"Guess he was out in the sun all day." The door slid slowly shut. "Don't worry, Jasuke. Your big brother will come round. No poisonous word scares this ex-journalist. We'll get you reading and writing in no time."

Numamushi smiled into his pillow, feeling like he'd basked on sun-warmed stone.

Maybe it could be this easy. Maybe, if just a little warmth, a little earth-steadiness could be found even in the dark house, some presence that didn't run or look away, something that could be bitten and stay unpoisoned. Even Mizukiyo, maybe even Mizukiyo could...

Numamushi opened his eyes.

No. This was snatching at frogs again, picking the tape-stuck mice.

Tora might not be afraid of any poisonous word, but that didn't matter when Mizukiyo was afraid enough for three.

Mizukiyo was venomous. The poison was already in his own mouth. He poisoned himself with it daily, with all the things he couldn't and shouldn't and wouldn't be and do. He was trying to hide his teeth like he hid his eyes behind his glasses, and in the hiding he had turned his bite inwards, away from the world, to bite his own tail.

The trouble wasn't Tora's fear. Tora wasn't afraid enough of Mizukiyo's poison to make Mizukiyo stop.

As sleep dragged him down, Numamushi decided. Tora had already seen Numamushi hunting once. It wouldn't make any difference being seen again. Mizukiyo needed to unsheathe his teeth, he needed to bite something that wasn't himself, and he needed to shed his skin—and for all of that, he needed to eat something that bled hot and living, not the sweet but dead rice Tora heaped in their bowls.

*W*HITE SNAKESKIN ROBES UNDER COTTON, Numamushi left Mizukiyo and Tora on their sleeping mats. The water in the paddy was murky from rainfall. It would take longer than usual to catch anything, but he didn't expect Mizukiyo to be awake for another hour, and Tora an hour after that.

Before he left, he touched Mizukiyo's forehead. Mizukiyo was clammy as a toad, warm and shivery.

"Father?"

Numamushi drew back.

"Are you cursing me, Father?" Mizukiyo spoke in the quiet voice of something that knew how to wait in the grass. "First a little brother. Now Tora. Are you cursing me to live?" He clenched his covers in his fists. "Ah, well, I suppose that's just what fathers and mothers do."

A crow called out and got no reply. Numamushi waited for Mizukiyo to speak again. When he didn't, he adjusted Mizukiyo's covers and stood.

Tora, asleep on Mizukiyo's other side, ground his teeth. For all his bright and easy words, his square face looked ready for a fight. Maybe Tora sensed something, even if he didn't know what. Numamushi tiptoed around him as carefully as he might a hornet's nest.

Heat lingered from the night in a wet fume. Numamushi finished his hunt as the morning star faded, and returned to the house with two frogs in each hand, a fifth between his teeth.

Tora was waiting on the veranda, arms folded and frowning hard at the persimmon tree. Spotting Numamushi, his frown softened.

He held out a bucket of water. "That's what Kiyo's been missing in his diet, is it?"

"They're not for you."

"I get it. Don't worry. I probably wouldn't appreciate the taste, anyway. Stick them in here, so they stay fresh for lunch." Numamushi narrowed his eyes. "I solemnly swear that I won't eat these delectable-looking amphibians. They're for Kiyo only."

Numamushi lowered the frogs into the bucket and charmed them. Once he'd spat out the last one and it landed with a splash, Tora spoke. "Jasuke, what would you say to you, me, and Kiyo leaving this old, dark house together?"

"Leave?" The word was suddenly as strange as if Mizukiyo had shown it to Numamushi in ink for the first time. "Why?"

"The same reason you're catching those frogs for him. You've realized, haven't you? Kiyo didn't come to this house to live here, as such."

Numamushi thought of Tora's mountain steadiness, his earthy gentleness, and told him the truth. "Niisan belongs to the land of the river, and the land of the river belongs to him."

"But he doesn't belong to the house?"

"No."

"So there's nothing keeping him in this house but his own stubborn hopelessness and self-loathing? So he could leave if the two of us convinced him?"

"The river—"

"The river's long, Jasuke." Tora crouched so as to look Numamushi in the eye. "This isn't the only patch of land it runs through. We don't need to stay here to stay with the river. Have you ever been to its wellspring in the mountain, Jasuke? Have you ever seen where it reaches the sea? It's the same river, but the lands and the winds and the waters running through them will all taste different. You should see all of it. Kiyo should see all of it." He looked to the room where Mizukiyo slept. "From what little I know of rivers, rivers are meant to flow. Not curl up in a spot and curdle."

Numamushi understood. "That's how a river dies."

"That's right. So, we're not going to let our Kiyo go that way, hm? He might have come to this house to do just that, to fade out after one last summer of decadent self-loathing and whatnot, but too bad for him! We'll match that loathing with everything we've got." Tora straightened, bucket of frogs sloshing, gaze clear. "So, what do you say to getting out of this house and finding somewhere for us three to live rather than letting Kiyo disappear?"

Numamushi recalled Father's stories of dark pines standing tall over the source spring, of the river mouth with its water saltier than blood. He thought of what it would be like to traverse Father's land from end to end, rather than keeping to the short span between the bridge and the dark house.

"I won't take him away from the river, Jasuke," said Tora gravely. "It's odd, but somehow, I think it helps him like himself more, like you do."

In the corner of Numamushi's eye, the shadows of the dark house seethed as if slugs and eels were buried in the eaves, dug in too deep to ever clean away. Father had said the land was poisonous, but the house had its own poison too. Soaked into the walls and the floors. Perhaps it was eating at Mizukiyo, now that he had played his part and delivered his mother's curse to Father.

Perhaps there was another curse here, meant to trap and kill Mizukiyo too.

Numamushi said, "Let's leave."

"Good!"

"Let's leave soon. Today. Now."

"Ha! Today might be a bit of a push, but you leave it to me! I'll get everything sorted. Now, we've just got to persuade your stone-headed brother." Tora looked over his shoulder into the house. "He's late getting up today. Towel down, Jasuke. Let's go and frighten the morning glories out of him."

Numamushi hurried to dry himself. He didn't want Mizukiyo frightened awake at all.

FAR FROM FRIGHTENING MIZUKIYO, Tora was on the floor when Numamushi had dried himself and returned, kneeling with a hand to Mizukiyo's forehead.

"I feel fine, Tora," Mizukiyo was slurring. He was still in bed. "Just a little warm with all this skin, that's all. There's nothing wrong with me."

"There is something wrong with him, isn't there?" Tora asked Numamushi, who was at a loss for what he could say or do that wouldn't make Mizukiyo upset at a time when he needed rest. "Jasuke, don't worry about your bully of a big brother. You can tell me."

"Jasuke." The mirror gleam of Mizukiyo's eyes was hidden under a milky blue film. "Tell Tora and I will bite you."

"Then you admit there is something wrong with you that Jasuke could tell me about?" Mizukiyo turned away with a hiss. Tora's face softened. "Let's find you a cold compress. Good thing you had an empty day ahead of you, our cursed local gentleman of leisure."

Mizukiyo curled in on himself, burying his head under the covers. Smile dimming, Tora gave Numamushi a look that promised more questions later, and left.

As soon as he was gone, Numamushi tugged at Mizukiyo's arm, found his hand, and prised open his fist. Sure enough, the skin at his fingertips had pulled back, translucent and pale, up to the bases of his second fingerbones. If Mizukiyo was sick and feverish, it was because he had been living in dead skin for a good half a month. Poisons accumulated in dead things, Father had always said so.

"Shed your skin."

"No."

"You'll feel better." Come to think of it, the house and its land were dead things too. Haunted and cursed things that were hurting Mizukiyo when he could shed them, leave them behind and go to the paddy or the river, where the waters were alive and clean. "You won't feel so warm."

"I said I'd never shed again."

"But then you won't grow. You won't have a new skin."

"I don't want a new skin. I don't want any of this anymore."

"What's wrong with new skins?"

"Humans aren't supposed to be able to just shuck off who they are, Numamushi, when they're sick of being themselves."

"I don't understand."

"Ask Tora to take you to the post office." Mizukiyo wrenched his hand from Numamushi, hiding it beneath his covers again. He had the limp, flattened look of a tree frog that had been smacked against the ground by its legs. "There's money in that drawer. There should be enough coins in there to buy a tin of peaches."

"Who's getting peaches?" Tora had returned with a damp cloth and a small bowl. Mizukiyo shuddered and curled deeper into his covers. "Nobody's leaving you here alone until I've said you're comfortable. Where's this fever come from anyway? Did you go rain-dancing in the night or something?"

"I thought I saw a rainbow last night."

"That's nice. I like rainbows. Jasuke does too, right, kid?"

Numamushi vehemently shook his head. Tora glanced between him and Mizukiyo before giving Mizukiyo a nudge. "Are you in pain?"

"No."

"Jasuke, bite your brother until he tells the truth."

"I'm in agony. I feel as if I'm being eaten alive by ants." Mizukiyo kept his eyes tightly shut, and Numamushi wondered if it was to hide the milky skin caps on his eyes or because the dead skin of his eyelids would tear if he opened them. "Just don't touch me, Tora. And leave me alone for the next hour. Then I'll be fine."

"This has happened before?"

"Yes," Mizukiyo said through gritted teeth, "and I survived every time, without you or Jasuke hovering next to me like nursemaid dragonflies who don't understand when they are not needed."

"No need to be snappish. All right. We'll leave our gentleman of leisure alone, then, as he requests." Tora laid the cloth over Mizukiyo's forehead, winning a sigh, and stood. "Let's just put another cover or two over you and get that fever sweated out. Jasuke, come and help me. Which one of these closets—?"

Tora's voice trailed to nothing. A smell, musty and sour with a sweetness like moldy straw, breathed into the room.

Numamushi looked up. The closet nearest to the door, the one painted with the snake people, which Numamushi had promised not to touch and pushed so far back and deep into the marsh of his mind he'd clean forgotten about it—it was open, and Tora stood with his hand frozen on the handle.

Inside were three bodies.

No, not three bodies. Three full-body skins. Old skin sheddings, but they weren't the empty inside-out peelings of long-empty arms and ribbony legs that Numamushi knew.

They were bodies made of paper-dry, moon-white skin, from hair to teeth to toes. They had eyeballs and bones and muscles of skin. One had its chest crushed open, and between the papery wads of scaly ribs was a scaly heart, chipped and flaking. They were dressed in faded clothes and their mouths were torn, splitting open their faces from ear to ear.

Three iterations of Mizukiyo's face stared out of the closet, and Tora and Numamushi stared back, until Tora finally shut the door.

"Wait." Mizukiyo pushed himself up, his arms shaking. "Tora, I can explain—"

"Just tell me one thing." Tora faced Mizukiyo. Numamushi suddenly wanted to crawl away and hide. "Are you Mizobata Mizukiyo, the man I went to war with, or has he died and been replaced?"

Mizukiyo opened his mouth. Tora stiffened as a long white tongue swept out of it to flicker at the air. "I don't know."

Tora swallowed. He nodded to himself. "All right. I see."

"What do you see?" Teeth were poised behind Mizukiyo's words. The hairs on the back of Numamushi's neck stood on end. "Is this something you can report to the police? To pest control? To a priest?" Mizukiyo held up his hand from the covers, lifted it to the light so that Tora could see the translucency of his palm. Bones, veins, and muscle had given way to honeycomb layers of skin, faintly patterned with scales like the pebbled bottom of a river bed. "If I could stay in this skin and die in it, kill the scum prison priest who fed his poison into the ears of all those men, I would, and I will. I came here to this house to do just that, to have one last summer where nobody was supposed see me being anything but this monster that I am! So that it'll all end where it started! But then there was you!" He pointed a shaking finger at Numamushi. "And you!" It went to Tora. "And you both had the nerve to look at me, and watch me, and ask me to continue living and being who and what you thought I was! How dare you! How dare you!"

Tora shook his head. "We never asked that of you."

Mizukiyo hissed. Tora jumped, stumbling back.

That movement seemed to shock them both. Mizukiyo's expression shuttered; Tora paled. They stared across the room at one another, stricken at the sudden distance.

Then Tora broke eye contact to look at his feet, as if incredulous that they'd moved of their own accord, and something shifted in the air.

Like a creep of coils. Like the pulling back of jaws for a blind, fearful bite, and Numamushi reached out quickly, just like he'd once reached for a falling frog. He wanted Mizukiyo to have choices, but this wasn't a choice, it was instinct, a snap of fear in the dark.

He grabbed Mizukiyo's head and forced the opening jaws shut.

"Niisan, don't," Numamushi said. "Don't use your poison. Don't bite."

"Poison?" repeated Tora, eyes round.

"Mizukiyo!" Numamushi urged his brother to listen, to hear the spell of his name. "Mizukiyo, please, don't be scared. Don't bite."

Mizukiyo writhed, clawing at Numamushi's head and arms, but in the end, Mizukiyo was weak from fever, and his control over this body was fading. His blows were uncoordinated and weaker than a frog's, and Numamushi could hold Mizukiyo's powerful jaws shut with his small bare hands.

"Listen," he said as Mizukiyo twisted and tried to snap his way free. "Listen to me. I'm the little brother, and I'm not scared. Listen."

He pressed Mizukiyo's head against his ribs and forced him to listen.

It was difficult not to be scared, but Numamushi thought of slugs and eels. He thought of the rainbow, the symbol of the river-killer, and traced it in his head. The river-killer was something that scared him. Mizukiyo wasn't. Tora wasn't. He drew the rainbow, he turned it to slugs and eels, soft black lines that he could flatten and roll in his palms and fingers. He focused on the river-killer and how small it could be when he drew it, how something so frightening as a river being killed could be shrunken to his fingertips, and drawn over and over again, until it was little more than a pattern and a rhythm that his heartbeats could follow.

His heartbeats, as he drew the rainbow, stayed steady.

"I'm not scared, see?" Numamushi said. Mizukiyo's movements slowed, his sharp ears filled with the thuds of Numamushi's heart. "Don't be scared, Niisan."

A shudder ran through Mizukiyo from head to toe.

Then, just as the pressure of Mizukiyo's jaw against Numamushi's hand eased, thunder clapped outside. Numamushi flinched; his grip loosened, and Mizukiyo tore his head from Numamushi's hold.

Tora cried out, throwing up his hands, but instead of attacking, Mizukiyo flung himself at the desk in the room's corner and snatched up a fistful of paper as pale and translucent as shed skin.

Mizukiyo stuffed the paper into his mouth. He crammed paper between his jaws until the corners of his lips split and tore. Then, biting down on the wad, Mizukiyo closed his eyes and screamed into it.

A black stain exploded from between his teeth, soaking into the paper and bleeding out to its edges. Mizukiyo screamed his muffled words into the paper, and the wad in his mouth dripped as if with ink. He tore up a third fistful, and a fourth, shoveling them into his mouth, and he kept on going until there were no more angry terrified words he could have bitten with, no more sounds, and everything had been drained into the paper and silence.

"Are you done?" Tora raised his hands as if to shield himself as Mizukiyo looked up wearily, ink-black sheets of paper stuffed between his teeth. "This is what you wanted me to see, right? This is...what you are. Well. I see. I see you. Whatever you are, I can handle it. I can handle this. Yes, I can handle this, just fine."

Tora swallowed thickly, took another backwards step. He looked at Numamushi.

He said, "Take care of him, Jasuke."

Then he fled, his footsteps echoing down the hallway.

Mizukiyo made not a sound. Black fluids dripped from the paper in his mouth to the desk. His eyes followed Tora out of the room.

Numamushi leapt up and ran after Tora. "Wait!"

Rain poured down grey and hard, land and sky blurring into one marbled sheet. The front door was open. The wind and water whipped against Numamushi's face as he pushed through it to call up and down the road. "Tora-nii! Tora!"

Tora was gone, his shadow and shape lost in a blue-grey wall of rain.

Numamushi's fingers curled into fangs. He swallowed the wet air, gulping it down. Tora had run from Mizukiyo like a mouse finding the mamushi in the gutter.

He wouldn't be coming back. Prey didn't come back after running like that, not until long after the predator was gone. Tora's face, the fear that had slackened his limbs and frozen his spine whilst Numamushi tried to stop Mizukiyo from striking, had been, indeed, the face of prey.

Numamushi turned. He stepped back inside the dark house and closed the door.

"Mizukiyo, Mizukiyo," he repeated, calling out the spell of a name. "Mizukiyo."

Mizukiyo was slumped over his desk, mouth stuffed with

sodden paper. He was watching thick black drops of his venom separate from the sheets and drip onto the tatami. They vanished without leaving a mark.

Picking up the damp cloth from where it had fallen, Numamushi knelt. He dabbed it over Mizukiyo's face, wiping sweat, then tears, then the tracks where saliva had oozed from the torn corners of Mizukiyo's mouth. Mizukiyo didn't look at him, didn't even move until Numamushi went to prise the venom-stained paper from his jaws, and then he finally lifted a feeble hand to push Numamushi's away.

Sheet by sheet, Mizukiyo pulled the paper from his mouth.

When all the stained paper lay in a torn pile on the desk, Mizukiyo looked up with red-rimmed eyes.

"The priest who raised me told me that words are water," he rasped. "Your voice when you speak them, your letters when you write them—those give your words shape and body. They hold the water of your words, as in a cup. The water becomes something that you can offer. Give someone as the purest gift. Water in a cup."

"Is that why you've only been teaching me symbols, but not how to join them together, to read and to write?" Numamushi asked. Thunder rolled again outside. "You've been teaching me about water, but not how to give it to people?"

"It's illogical, isn't it? You can already speak. I can't take your voice from you, but I was so afraid that you were like me, and Father had simply kept you unaware of it..." Mizukiyo raised a hand blindly. The eyes of this body had died. Numamushi stayed still and let the hand search for and find the side of his face. Mizukiyo's touch was warm

with fever. He dug around the hinge of Numamushi's jaw where Numamushi had always lamented his lack of venom pouches. "I did wonder if I ought to bite out your tongue, for your sake, just in case, so that you'd never need worry about hurting anybody you cared for."

"You said you'd hurt me if I opened the closet."

"You were only able to stop me because I'm sick and slow. I've done it before, Numamushi. Twice. I'd snap, and there would be poison in the water of my words, this very poison you see in this paper, and suddenly my words are venom in the blood. There was a man at the temple. And at the camp... one went mad and the other...ah, you don't need to know." Mizukiyo's hand moved from Numamushi's jaw to ruffle his hair, but the gesture was half-hearted. "You must be wondering why I taught you anything about words at all, even if it was just to draw them."

Numamushi looked at the sodden pile of poisoned paper and shook his head. "Family shares everything, especially the sad things."

"Ah."

"Tora's gone."

"Yes, he is, isn't he? At long last." Mizukiyo lowered his hand to the desk. "Did I ever show you the symbol for *poison*, Numamushi?"

He dipped his forefinger into the stained paper mound, coated it in the blackness, and drew on the table surface, layering the strokes so that they lingered, thick and glistening.

"You'd think it'd have origins in something like a snake or a wasp, but it came from neither. See how it has two halves? The lower half—" Mizukiyo lightly covered the top, the river of his voice wavering. "Some say it represents *mother*. It's a kneeling woman with breasts for suckling. The top half is a gaudy hairpiece. You wouldn't know what a hairpiece is, would you? You didn't even know the days of the week when we first met. Not the year, not the name of the Emperor. Well, apparently, a woman wearing a gaudy, excessively large hairpiece was unsuitable for the woman's work of communicating with the gods, and that's where our symbol for *poison* comes from—from a mother offending the gods. From an unwelcome, unwanted, arrogant woman, and her stupid, arrogant choices."

"Niisan—"

"But, well, I shouldn't be so uncharitable. That's only one theory, of course. There's another that says it comes from a combination of *grass* and then the picture of a human who's lost all control of their limbs." The symbol shimmered darkly and vanished. Mizukiyo laid his head down over where it disappeared. "Father didn't know as much about humans as he thought, Numamushi. He might've known many things, but not enough about them. He told you that humans didn't make poison in their mouths and that it wasn't human to make it. He was wrong. Humans have their poison too. They put it in the water of their words without knowing and turn those words into medicines and poisons as they need and see fit. I am only different in that I deliver my poison with a snake's knowledge that it is there, in my mouth, for me to use, and a snake's instincts to bite with it, and no word of mine will ever be able to heal a human. If only all-knowing Father had known that, maybe he would've liked humans a little less, and you and I wouldn't be as we are."

"Mizukiyo." Numamushi took Mizukiyo's hands, warm with fever, stiff as frozen birch. Thunder boomed. "Niisan, let's leave."

"Leave? Oh, yes, you're right...Tora would have gone to fetch someone, wouldn't he? Who do you think he'll go to? Who would have a large enough hand-sickle to cut off this snake's head?"

"Let's go away from here."

"And go where?"

"To the river."

The corners of Mizukiyo's torn mouth turned up. "To live in the emptied house of another parent I killed?"

"It's a different river now." The rain had made the river louder, so Numamushi could hear it clearly. The foam it stirred up, the water under the bridge, was new yet familiar. New words were being chanted in an old voice. It wasn't Father's river anymore. It could be theirs. "You won't be haunted. You won't be cursed."

"Maybe I should send you away to live in your precious river alone," Mizukiyo said, poison tucked behind his tongue, "so you'll never come back to curse me to live again."

"I've never cursed you."

"No. No, you're right. I'm sorry, I'm so sorry. It was Father. It was all Father." Mizukiyo fell silent. "This body is almost entirely dead. I can't move it, unless I..."

Shed it.

Numamushi said nothing. He wouldn't take that choice from Mizukiyo. He picked up the damp cloth again, dipped it in the small bowl of water Tora had left, and patted it over Mizukiyo's fever-hot neck and shoulders. If Mizukiyo was feeling small and scared, Numamushi couldn't be either. He fought down his instincts to flee and hide, traced the river-killer rainbow in his mind, and kept his heartbeats steady.

Listen, Mizukiyo. Don't be scared.

The river roared, louder and louder.

It sounded closer than before. Numamushi went to the veranda door. He had barely opened the shutter a thumb's width before the wind and rain drove him back into the room.

Raindrops stung his eyes. Through the narrow gap, he saw a dark grey sheet of water pouring over the paddy.

The river had burst its banks.

It sprawled across the paddy, groping towards the house in a many-fingered arc, forming a muddy hand at the end of a narrow grey arm that stretched from beneath the bridge. It flowed in a direct course to the dark house only, creeping into the allotment to lap at the steps.

When the hand of the river reached the steps, it spread into an open palm, gently offering.

With a smile, Numamushi turned to Mizukiyo. Mizukiyo let out a sigh. "I should've known better than to have agreed to take care of you so easily."

"Niisan?"

"Don't worry, little one." Mizukiyo closed his eyes and hooked a finger into the corner of his mouth. "First a little brother. Then Tora. All right. As you wish, Father. I'll shoulder this curse of yours. I'll take it. I'll bear it. I'll take your curse for them. And for us."

He ripped his mouth open to his ears, and shed his skin.

The angular face of a white snake nosed out of Mizukiyo's mouth. It was Mizukiyo, climbing out of his dead human skin, ribs gripping the weave of the floor as he emerged, coil after rippling coil. The body he was leaving paled from the head downwards, turning flaky and scaled like the skins in the closet as he cast it off.

The white snake Mizukiyo's head was smaller than Father's, but its shape and color was just the same. Numamushi reached out and hugged it tight, hoping that Mizukiyo would hear his heartbeats and know not to be afraid.

Mizukiyo breathed through his nose, slit nostrils flaring. A long white tongue flickered between clenched teeth. He was still hot from fever and shivered in the air and sprays of rain coming in through the open veranda door.

Coil upon coil followed until Mizukiyo lay stretched across the floor, long white body filling the room. In moments, a transformation began. Thin tendrils of white budded along the snake's body, stretching into the spindly forms of human arms and legs. The head Numamushi was holding became defined and rounded, its eye sockets deepening, its jaw shrinking. Thin wisps of skin sprouted, darkened, and curled into hair.

"Mizukiyo, Mizukiyo," Numamushi repeated, patting the cheek with its venom. "There, there. I'll never let you be lost again. Mizukiyo."

That was how Tora found them when he returned: Mizukiyo's body halfway back to human, Numamushi wiping the rain off his face as it blew sideways into the room. Numamushi had left the veranda door open, so that Mizukiyo could see the hand of the river as it waited with offered shelter. Neither realized that Tora was there until the man's weight made the tatami creak at the doorway.

Numamushi shrank back, shielding Mizukiyo. Jostled by the movement, Mizukiyo opened his eyes.

"Tora." Mizukiyo's human throat was still new, his vocal cords tender. "Where's your Kusanagi sword, Tora?"

"What are you talking about?" Rainwater dripped off Tora's hat and coat. His gaze was warm, even if his eyes were blood-shot and a little too wide. "You think I'm here to end you? I just had the fright of my life watching you cough up ink, thinking you were about to die of some mystical snakish illness, and I'd be too late!"

"Too late for what?" Numamushi asked uncertainly.

Digging into his inner coat pocket, Tora pulled out a crumpled paper bag. He tossed it up and down in one hand. "Anti-fever. Painkillers. Kiyo's taken these ones before, so half-snake, half-human, all god or demon, we know they work on him."

Mizukiyo stared. Numamushi tightened his grip on his

brother, reminding Mizukiyo that he didn't need to bite, that he didn't need to use his poison to be safe. At their silence, Tora's smile shriveled.

He set the bag on the desk, a careful distance from the heap of poisoned paper, and cleared his throat. "How are you feeling, Kiyo?"

"I told you that I didn't know if I was the Mizukiyo you knew or not."

"Which is exactly the answer the Mizukiyo I know would give." Tora's eyes were wet and bright. "I told you not to leave me here. Not to disappear from this world like the others. I don't care how you stay in it, or what shape you are, or whether you go through paper bodies like a candle in a lantern. I just need you here. If not for me, then for your little brother. For a moment back there, I got scared that you'd been gone all along, that the one I was seeing in front of me was either a ghost or all in my head or a stranger who'd kept me from mourning like I should have been, maybe out of pity or kindness—I wouldn't dare guess."

Mizukiyo raised a hand. It was still pearl-white, still pebbled with scales. Tora clasped it between his two rain-drenched hands and bowed his head, pressing his lips to their knuckles.

"I'm going to get you out of this cursed house," he said. "I've already talked about it with Jasuke. He says he's good with it."

"What about the river?"

"It's here to help you," Numamushi said, more familiar with the whisper of the water than Mizukiyo was.

"Thirty minutes before their execution, I took men into a little room, read them sutras, lit them incense, and gave them grape wine." Mizukiyo looked Tora in the eye with a challenge. "They sang '*Tennouheika banzai*' and I shook all their hands, smiled, told them that I wished them all the very best. That's when I put my poison in their ears to kill their minds, and keep them dumb and calm right up to the noose."

"And they're all dead and you're still alive, and I'm so glad that's the way it is, however unfair you might think it. Let's leave, Kiyo. Let all this go," Tora said, glancing at the dark eaves above, the painted walls of closets. "Live with Jasuke and me. We'll keep the river in our life. There's a whole life to be had living along it, a moving, flowing life. Besides, this old house is done for with the river getting under it. Think of that repair bill."

Mizukiyo grimaced. "I'd rather not."

The river water rose. It nudged at the veranda's edge. Mizukiyo looked at it, mirror eyes catching the silver light of the stormy day. He turned to Numamushi. "You say it's here to help me?"

"Yes."

Something settled in Mizukiyo's expression. His eyes went to his closet of skins.

"Numamushi, would you open that for me?"

THE RIVER WITHDREW. As the storm ended and the sun emerged, the water carried four snakeskin bodies into a hollow where once there had been a home.

In the quiet and the cold, they dissolved. Dead skin vanished into the flow of the river. In the water of the river's words, the poison of the past scattered, became moonlight scales floating with a trace of mirror gleam.

*I*N A NEW HOUSE along the river, there was a boy that was snake and human. He lived well and happily. Some days he could be lost, which was only to be expected for humans, but he had his family to call his name, just as they had him to do the same for them.

"The symbol for river is easy," his brother said on a dark night of the mind, the kind of night when it was good to think upon the trusting act that was loving. He drew three strong strokes. (川) "See? It flows on the page."

"That's us," said the other brother, "when we sleep at night. Little Numamushi in the middle. Kiyo on the left. Me, the log on the right."

"Some log you are. If only you'd sleep like one!"

Once the boy had learnt to read and write, he asked, because he would never not be cautious with slugs and eels, "Niisan, does this mean that Tora's taught me how to make venom?"

"He did no such thing," his brother replied. "We humans are born venomous. He's only taught you the cups and tumblers—the ways that words can be offered and shared between us. How you put your venom in the water of your words is up to you."

ACKNOWLEDGMENTS

*T*HIS STORY BEGAN WITH A SNAKE in a ditch, something yellowy brown and sluggish in the summer heat. I stopped on the concrete footbridge when its movement caught my attention and its eye flashed at me—probably the sun on the water at the ditch bottom, but it looked to me like a mirror sequin. My first acknowledgment for this story will be to the snake.

My second acknowledgment should be to folklorist Yoshino Yuuko and her work regarding snake worship, snake folklore, and theories regarding snakes and culture in Japan. I don't agree with all of her theories, but I respect the possibility of them. I found her on Google searches because her observation that "snake eye" (*kaga no me*) was a potential word origin for "mirror" (*kagami*) matched my own impression of the snake's eye in the dark ditch. I owe much to her book *Hebi: Nihon no Hebi Shinkō* (*Snakes: Japan's Snake Worship*, 1999), as much of the information I could find on the topic online seemed to have been rooted in this work, and to the snakes in the Japanese culture blog JANONET123.COM.

For word origins, GOGEN-YURAI.JP was another useful resource.

A huge thank you must go to the team at Lanternfish Press, who flipped over all my expectations by choosing to invest their time and faith in this story—so to Christine, Feliza, and Amanda, and those I haven't had the pleasure of corresponding with, thank you to all you guys over in the States who took a chance on my snake boy story. It's been a ride.

Thank you to Ambre Morvan for her good work at the Society of Authors; to Eva Wong Nava, who read this and gifted me with her kind words; and to all you folks of Bubble Tea Writers Network: thank you for your warm support throughout my ups and downs with writing.

Lastly, to my family and my friends, to my people of choice: you are dear to me, and the world is easier to like with you all in it.

About the Author

MINA IKEMOTO GHOSH is a British-Japanese writer and illustrator, born and raised in between two worlds. Shortlisted twice for the UK Manga Jiman, she writes speculative shorts and draws sad monsters. She lives in Surrey, UK, fumbling through life, and with her words.